T0278647

# DEATH'S
## COUNTRY

Published by Peachtree Teen
An imprint of PEACHTREE PUBLISHING COMPANY INC.
1700 Chattahoochee Avenue
Atlanta, Georgia 30318-2112
*PeachtreeBooks.com*

Text © 2024 by R. M. Romero
Jacket illustration © 2024 by Carolina Rodriguez Fuenmayor

Edited by Ashley Hearn
Design and composition by Lily Steele

Printed and bound in March 2024 at Sheridan, Chelsea, MI, USA.
10 9 8 7 6 5 4 3 2 1
First Edition
ISBN: 978-1-68263-691-6

Cataloging-in-Publication Data is available from the Library of Congress.

R. M. ROMERO

# DEATH'S COUNTRY

PEACHTREE
*Teen*

*For anyone who has ever*
*braved the underworld*

"I am the way to go among the lost."

—Dante Alighieri, *The Divine Comedy*

# CANTO I
## AS ABOVE

# PROLOGUE

**The most important lesson I've learned**
since I turned sixteen:
Love can't be contained
in a word, a kiss, a single heart.

Love's a pandemonium of parakeets,
free and bright.
Love isn't a single beat; it's a serenade,
one line rolling into the next.
Love can be stretched like toffee
across bodies and lips.
Love won't shatter when it's held
in more than one hand.

Love doesn't need to be divided
between only two people.
There's enough of it
to go around.

So I'm not afraid of letting love in.
I'm afraid of letting it drag me down,
       down,
down,
back into
the underground.
Which is exactly where love
is trying to take me tonight.
(If I have the courage
to follow it.)

# CHAPTER
## ONE

**Every hospital reeks of distilled sadness;**
Mount Sinai in Miami Beach
is no different.

As me and my girlfriend Renee
escaped its halls,
I gulped in the night air, clearing the dead-dream rot
from my lungs.

Renee's hand was wrapped
tightly in mine, a gift I didn't want to surrender.
My other hand was
(strangely)
empty.

But that emptiness was the reason
we stood
under the Cheshire cat grin of the moon,
carrying
the burning afterimage of our girlfriend
in her hospital-room-turned-tomb
as 2 AM
bled into 3.
We were a fractured pair
when we were meant to be
a trio.

And it was all because of the foolish bargain
I'd made
while living in a city divided
by two rivers—
one of which had tried to swallow me
whole.

# CHAPTER
## TWO

**I can't remember why I fractured Eduardo's jaw**
in the courtyard of Escola Maria Imaculada.
(Home of the best education
money could buy
in twenty-first century Brazil.)

Did Eduardo stare at me
for a breath too long?
Did his shadow cross mine
when I was enjoying my solitude?

Whatever the reason for my fury,
I only remember
the firecracker burst of my fist
as it connected with Eduardo's face,
the thunderclap of his skull
as it struck the marble walkway.

I only remember
how the other boys circling us
                    STOPPED
their chant
          (*Fight, fight, fight!*)
when the dry snap of bone
bellowed through the searing summer air.
To them, a brawl
was the means to solve problems,
not create new ones—and I
          just
had.

Snarling, I tackled Eduardo.
Our bodies collided, the impact
shaking
the hills of our city and the watchful houses
perched on their peaks.

I was Andres Santos of São Paulo.
And on that day, I wore two faces
in honor of my home: the jaguar and the prince.

But the prince
was no kinder than the beast.
His cruelty and cleverness were only slightly
*different*.

**Every fairy tale ends with a prince.**
The princess's adventure in the wild woods
is finished by his wedding ring.
The dragon's life among its hard-won treasure
is cut short at the tip of his sword.
The old king's golden reign
fades to history
thanks to his bravery and youth.

So when I say I was a prince,
I don't mean I was a hero.

I mean
I took what I wanted from others
before they could take it from *me*.

**After the principal hauled me**
off Eduardo, across the courtyard, into his office,
I smoothed my hair into an oil slick,
straightened my collar,
replaced my snarl with a grin,
café-com-leite sweet.

*I've had enough of you,*
*Santos!* the principal bellowed,
as loud as my fists had been.
*No more forgiveness!*
*No more second chances!*
*This time, you're out of my school—*
*for good!*

He reached for the phone
        (a threat to my future
        lying in wait)
on his desk.

Another boy
might have thrown himself at the man's feet,
kissed his ring, begged for a third chance.
But I was too good at pretending
        blood wasn't drying to my knuckles
                and shame wasn't burning in my belly
to sink so low.

I reminded the principal,
*My parents won't be happy*
*if you do.*
*They might even sue.*
*Not the school, but you . . .*
*personally.*
*And really, how much do you make*
*as a school principal?*

The specter of a lawsuit
stole the furious color
from the principal's cheeks.
He crumbed, his power fading
as his hand retreated
farther and farther from the phone.

*You're suspended*
*for two days,* the principal wheezed out.
*And I'll have to call your parents*
*at the very least.*

I shrugged
to show
what I thought of *that.*

(Princes could endure temporary banishment.)

**Mami arrived to collect me less than an hour later**
in her queenly regalia:
heels reaching halfway to Heaven,
her face schooled to severe perfection
thanks to years of practice
in front of the camera.

We left the school grounds
        (every wall and gate
        carved from white marble
        to hold back the December heat)
chased by a pack of whispers.

*Andres Santos.*
        *Oh,* him.

*His handsome papi is Brazilian.*
*Senhor Santos might be the boto cor de rosa,*
*the enchanter*
*who crawls out of the river*
*and undoes women with his charms.*

> *He must have given up*
> *being a folktale then.*
> *Because now he sells castles and mansions*
> *to men whose money*
> *makes them kings.*

*Look, that's his Cuban mami!*
*She used to be the queen of telenovelas,*
*the beautiful, burning heart*
*of every beloved story.*

> *Now she's made of*
> *too much makeup, too many teardrops.*

*Andres Santos can make any girl*
*kiss him.*

> *He can break any boy*
> *(like poor Eduardo!)*
> *with his fists.*

*He can dance storms*
*to life.*

*He draws poison in*
*and out of wounds.*

But my heart
was too riddled with bullet holes
to care
about the bite of any classmate's words.

**Mami held off wailing like a mourner**
until we were safely in her car.
*Next time,*
*you'll surely be expelled!* she cried,
weeping
a third river to join São Paulo's other two.
*You're too much*
*like your father!*
*He bites*
*his way through the world,*
*kisses women*
*like he wants to break them.*
*If you're not careful,*
*you're going to end up*
   *just*
     *like*
*him!*

A signal flare of anger
crackled
in my chest.
What Mami had said about my father
was (mostly) true—
but I didn't want to be a foot soldier
in their war, forced to take a side
when neither of them
was ever on mine.

I couldn't let Mami
hear my bitterness, so I let a lullaby lilt
creep into the reassurances
I offered her.

*Papi's not so bad*, I said.
*And don't worry about me.*
*I was angry at a classmate.*
*But I promise,*
*it won't happen again.*

Mami dabbed at her radiant tears.
Some were prepackaged; others might have been real.
It was hard to tell.
*You and your father never keep*
*your promises!*

*Mami*— I began.

But she had already crushed my face
in her hands.

>                   (She was always trying to crush me
>                   into some boy, some shape, some soul
>                   I couldn't be.)

*I was somebody*

>                   *(somebody happy!)*

*before I married your father!* Mami told me.
*Remember that.*
*Keep your promises, and don't let love*
*eat you up*
*like it's eaten* me.

**Papi shimmied home too late that night.**
Dinner had gone cold; Mami's fury hadn't.
It was red as the dawn
sailors fear.

She followed Papi through our house,
(the rooms sleek, hollow, empty)
her hands conducting
her anger.
*You can't even bother*
*to be here for your son!*
*You're too busy*
*with your money, your girlfriends, your*self!

Papi rolled his eyes
like he rolled his hips
when he danced.
*Why should I*
*come home from work early*
*because Andres got in a fight?* he asked.
*Boys fight!*
*And it shows Andres will grow up*
*to be a strong man.*
Papi tipped his hat
            (and a wink)
my way.
*That is,*
*if you won.*

I *always* won.
But one look from my Mami
silenced my would-be boast.

*Go*, she said.
            *To your room*, Papi finished.

I slunk away, half grateful
they were still together enough to issue
joint commands.

**Like many fifteen-year-olds, I breathed and bled**
music.
Cut me open and you'd find
David Bowie, Billie Eilish, Arcade Fire
scratched on my eyelids and arteries.

With my parents busy
firing insults and past grievances
at each other,

> *(You playboy!*
> *I know why*
> *you're really home*
> *so late!*

> *I was working—unlike you,*
> *you useless leech, you has-been!)*

I retreated to bed, snapped my headphones on,
and sank
into the music,
like I'd sink
into a river or a sea.
Jimi Hendrix
("All Along the Watchtower," 1968)
begged for a way
out of here.

And so did I.
I prayed
to whatever god would have me:
*Let me be*
*a whisper of music, the calm inside the storm.*
*Let me be someone* better.

But that night, no spirits
heard my pleas, and I stayed a snarl
of thorns playacting
at being a boy.

**During my suspension,**
Papi took me to his office—a reward and a punishment
fused into a single outing.

I was the jaguar for him,
lean and well muscled.
I strutted past his colleagues,
the first two buttons of my collar
thrown open in welcome,
my gold chain winking
flirtatiously at the secretaries.

Papi slapped me on the back, congratulating *himself*
on the boy he'd decided I was.
He told his business partners,
his not-so-secret girlfriend,
other men on the street:

*This is my son, Andres.*
*He's everything, isn't he?*
*Smart, fierce,*
*good at sports, good with girls.*
*He'll inherit*
*my business, my legacy*
*when I'm gone.*

But behind my smiles, I plotted
my tomorrows,
my flight from the inheritance
Papi wanted to pour into my hands.

In the end, my escape attempt
was more effective
than I ever could have hoped.

# CHAPTER
## THREE

**We weren't supposed to swim in the Tietê River.**
Our parents, aunts, grandfathers warned us
it was too wild, too choked with the pollution
we'd been shoving in its mouth
for decades.

But I didn't care.

I texted
every boy whose number I had, demanding
they join me at the riverbank.
After Eduardo,
none of them argued; none of them refused
to play my game.
(No matter how dangerous.)

My fearful congregation
gathered at the Tietê on Sunday afternoon.

They shuffled their tan, sandaled feet,
hid their eyes from my blistering grin.

I stepped up to challenge the swift waters,
taunting the tides
like they could never rule *me*.
*I can make it to the other side!* I crowed
at my witnesses.
*Who will join me?*

No one else
moved.

*Cowards!* I laughed and threw myself into the bleak
brown water.
I swam
as far, as *fast* as I could
from São Paulo, my parents, every mistake
I'd left like a bruise
on the life of another.
But my strength was nothing
compared to the Tietê's.

Its muddy hands
            gripped
                        me
by the ankle, tearing me
out of the sun-dappled world.

*You'll never beat* me, *Andres Santos!* the river cackled.
*But I*
*have beaten* you.

**If black is all colors combined,**
true darkness
was something else.
It went on
halfway past forever, filling my wounds
as it took me deeper
        and
                deeper.

And when the darkness
faded to gold
and the roar of the Tietê became an echo
humming between worlds,
I knew exactly
where I'd arrived.

There were no road signs in that place;
it would never be on any map.
But I *felt* what it was—
a flagging pulse, a clock winding down,
the final page in the last book
ever written.

I was in Death's country,
where the path ends for everyone.

**Death's country was all roses and marigolds,**
its sky bejeweled with ghostly stars.
Their light burned the Tietê
right off my shoulders and chest.
But drops of the river
clung to my lips, eager to travel
down into my lungs.

Spirit children
danced in the flowers, carrying kites and candles
offered by the living
on feast days.

The ocean of marigolds
eventually joined with a true river.
Its frothing waters flowed past a wood
        bathed in shadows
and up to a dark city skyline.
Its high towers were cloaked
in a shroud of rain.
No stars twinkled above it;
they refused to lend their light
to that strange place.

The names of the city
        (dozens, hundreds)
filled my head, and so did its songs:

a funeral dirge, a choked sob,
a plea for one
       more
           word
                and
          one
       more
minute.

But I was more concerned with Death
herself.

**They call her:**
Holy Bone Mother.
They call her:
the Grim Reaper, eternal sleep.
They call her:
Azrael, *malakh ha-mavet*, the most fearsome angel.

We all have to call her
some*thing*, because she greets us all
some*day*.
My audience with her
just happened to be earlier
than I (or anyone else) expected.

**Death came to greet me,**
her robe a wave of eventide tulle,
her smile sharp as my temper,
her scythe silver as a gutted moon.

To face Death
is to glimpse the whole of your life.
And as she closed in on me,
I heard
every muffled shriek into my pillow,
tasted
every tear I'd refused to cry,
felt
every blow I'd delivered to someone else's belly.

In Death's empty eyes, I saw
a parade of barren kisses, hollow friendships,
Mami and Papi's claws ripping at me.
*Be good, be clever, be better, be stronger*
*than your playboy father,*
*than your weeping mother!*

I hung my head as low
as I believed my grave would be,
the river and my tears
a single current.
*I wasted it, didn't I?* I rasped.
*I wasted my life*
*being angry—*
*at my parents, at the world.*

*You lived*, Death replied.
*That was no waste.*
*And you will* continue *to live.*
*You're not done yet, little prince.*

**My knees gave way in the marigolds,**
and I clutched at the hem of Death's dress,
fifteen years
> (of laughter and screams,
> of relief and *dread*)
bearing down on me.

*You're greater*
*than anything else!* I said to Death.
*You arrive*
*on the corner of every street*
*and the door of every home*
*eventually.*
*So your miracles*
*must be boundless too.*

I brought Death's skirt
up to my lips,
pressing my pleas into the rippling tulle.
*Please*, I begged.
*If I have to go*
*back to my life, to the world,*
*make me better than I was!*
*Make me* good!

(A true prince would never seek mercy
from anyone.
But I didn't want to be a prince
ever again.)

Death shrugged.
Her shoulders were the scales of justice,
but they didn't tip in one direction
or the other.
*What is good?* she asked.
*One action leading to another?*
*One kindness creating a second?*
*I don't know.*
*I'm not here to judge*
*the cyclone lash of your temper,*
*the weight of your fears.*
*Before me, everyone is equal;*
*all requests are considered.*
*(But not always granted.)*

*Then I ask you—*
*please take the anger*
*out of me!* I cried.
*Bury it*
*where it can't hurt me . . .*
*or the people* around *me.*
*I'm tired of being*
*this person, this boy, this* mess.

*And what will you give* me
*in exchange?* Death inquired.

I wrenched away from her . . .
and my own confusion.
But I shouldn't have been
so surprised.
Death is transactional by nature;
offer her your bones
and she'll grow a banyan forest from them.

I dug my hands into the flowers,
trying to unearth the courage
for my last question.
*What do you want?*

Death's fingers
played a samba on her scythe
as she considered.
*I am balance; I make all things*
*equal.*
*If I take away*
*something you* hate,
*you must give me*
*something you* love *in return.*

The river
tightened its cold fists around my throat.
*Something I love?*

*At this moment, you don't love anything*
*enough for me to claim it*, said Death.
*But if we strike a bargain,*
*I will come to collect*
*what belongs to me someday.*

It's never good to owe a favor
when the price hasn't been named.
But in Death's country,
             choking on my life and foul water,
I wanted to take the risk;
I wanted to be *different*.

*Take the anger out of me*, I whispered to Death.
*If you do that, I'll give you*
*whatever you want,*
*whenever you want it.*

                And Death
                whispered back,
                *Done.*

**Under the world, under the river,**
Death raised her scythe and cleaved away
my shadow.

It unraveled
from the tips of my toes,
spilling
like blood across the marigolds.

My shadow stared at me as it fell away,
its eyes damp
with tears of its own.
*Traitor, traitor, traitor!* my shadow howled.

But it wasn't guilt or grief I felt
as I watched my shadow go.
It was the warm rush of sunlight
     and
          relief.

My soul swam back to life, and the Tietê left me,
drop by drop.

# CHAPTER
## FOUR

**Death had changed me; everyone sensed the shift.**
And it guided
the whispers of my classmates, my teachers,
the men on the street.

*Andres Santos,*
>  *Oh,* him.

*After all this time, he finally lost*
*a fight!*
*Now his ego's sandcastle fragile.*

>  *I heard his heart stopped*
>  *when the Tietê put him in his place.*

*He's nothing*
*to be afraid of these days.*

I let the rumors
wash over me, half muted by Pink Floyd, the Who,
drum solos, the ripple of guitar strings
on my headphones,

How could I tell anyone
about Death
and the invisible weight of her scythe
hanging over me?

The answer:
I couldn't.

**Two months after I left the land of the dead**
and turned sixteen,
my parents called a temporary truce,
abandoning their frontlines
in São Paulo
and signing an armistice
in Miami Beach.

Papi grabbed Mami by the waist, declaring,
*We'll have*
*a new beginning!*
*I'll expand my business*
*so it can stretch across whole continents!*
*And we'll all be happy.*

Mami kissed the words from his mouth,
like she could make them true
if she caught them
on her own lips.
*Change can be difficult*, she said.
*But it can also be necessary.*

I nodded along.
I wasn't sad to be leaving São Paulo,
which had flooded me
with a tributary of scars.
I had a new life now;
it was only fitting I'd have a new country
to go with it.

**Miami was a young city, founded in 1896.**
It enjoyed its adolescence,
prolonged its teenage dreams.
There, skyscrapers grew like cypress trees;
art galleries and murals spread like beach sunflowers.

Developers and real estate agents
    (like Papi)
encouraged the city to grow.
They ignored
the king tides, the flooded streets,
the summers that made the pavement bubble.

The end of the world ran wild
in Miami.
And it would soon run wild
in my family's home.

**My parents welcomed me to Miami**
with a present:
an electric Strat guitar, sleek and whale-belly
blue.

I recognized the yellow scent
of a guilt gift; it wasn't the first one
I'd received.
But I still pulled the guitar close
the moment it was offered.

How could I refuse
the chance to transform what was inside me
using six strings and chords?

*We're sorry*
*about the past few months,*
*how stressed we've been,*
*how difficult this transition is,*
my parents said,
in concert with each other.
*Things will be better from now on—*
*and you can have a wonderful fresh start*
*in this city.*

*Thank you*, I murmured.
I couldn't bring myself to believe
Mami and Papi's lies
about themselves.
But Death had made me believe
          (just a little)
in my own future.


**Within a few weeks, my parents' war resumed**,
the carnage worse than ever.
They rattled the walls of our new house,
their weapons
far more than words this time.


Mami put Papi's name in her left shoe,
tapping it whenever he angered her;
Papi scribbled hers on a slip of paper
before dousing it
in lime and vinegar.
They cursed each other
          (*Puedes hincharte de desesperación;*
          swell with despair!
                    *Que sua vida seja amarga;*
                    may your life be bitter!)
a hundred times over.


I rejected the folk magic
my parents invoked
and hid in my room, trying to mask
their battle cries with music
of my own.

I built an empire of calluses
on the pads of my fingers,
new aches and muscles on my wrists
as I got to know my guitar,
her major Fs, minor Es.

But however many songs we made together,
my guitar refused to tell me
her name.

*I am, I am, I am*, her heartstrings murmured,
without ever finishing the thought.

I loved her anyway.

**Hurricanes don't hit Miami till August.**
But the finale of my parents' fractured marriage
came in a June storm of allegations—
all of them true.

Mami was done with magic;
she threw her diamond ring at Papi,
her tears falling like bits of broken glass
he was careful to avoid.
*I saw the messages
on your phone!* Mami screamed.
*I know you have another girlfriend!
Get out,*

*get out,*
*GET OUT!*

Papi packed up his life
            (Gucci loafers, Armani suits,
                two computers, and a scowl)
and slapped me on the back, the closest thing to a hug
he'd allow himself to give.
*You're the man of the house now*, Papi said.
*Don't let your mother*
*turn you soft.*

What could I possibly say
to *that*?
Staring at my father's grin
            (big enough to split his face
                and part the sea)
I almost missed the anger
that had lit up my heart
in São Paulo.
How *dare* Papi tell me to be a man
when he was such a poor one
himself?

*Papi*, I tried. *Stay.*
*Just apologize to Mami.*
*She'll forgive you; she always does.*

Papi shook his head to a runaway's tune.
*Not this time, Andres.*
*I'll call you*
*when I have a new place.*

Then he left
the way all shadows do: quietly, only darkening
the corners of the day.

I could have stayed, held Mami,
assured her
she could reclaim her happiness
now that Papi was gone.
But my shoulders had already caved
under the weight of the day.
I wasn't in any shape to let any*one*
lean on me.

I followed the pull of the wind
out the door,
my guitar slung over one shoulder
in place of a prince's sword.

# CHAPTER
## FIVE

**The tip of Miami Beach was home to**
a rainbow of lifeguard towers, a few tourists,
and a kingdom of feral cats.
I joined these strays as they prowled
over the pier, across the jetty, onto the sand.

The cats watched me
with marigold-bright eyes.
They must have known I'd been like them once,
full of predatory grace.

As I walked, my shirt
stuck
to my skin like bubble gum;
I wrenched it off, escaping the humidity.

The thick scars on my chest
formed a path, traveling up from my death
      (in the blue depths of the river)
to my life.
      (In Miami.)

The scars were songs too, in their own way.
Who said every piece of music
had to be *brigadeiro* sweet,
an anthem told only in smooth syllables?

**I shielded my eyes from the sinking sun**
and looked

           out
           to
           sea.

The borders of the island were defined
by something greater
than a human hand.

According to Mami,
it was Yemaya,
the mermaid goddess, the mother of all oceans,
who created them.

Gods have always traveled with more ease
than people.

They ride wind and waves,
slip past guards, dictators,
chain-link fences, hostilities between nations.
They don't need passports;
they only need belief.

So maybe it was my belief
in Yemaya that summoned her daughters:
two girls
waist-deep in the sea.

The ocean embraced the first girl
        (the narrow curve of her hips,
          the ends of her snow-bright hair,
          her hands that danced like dragonflies)
more gently than any body of water
had ever held *me*.

The waves lapped more roughly
at the second girl, who held her camera
high.
She snapped photos of her companion,
the lens taking in
how the sunset rolled
off the other girl's shoulders,
how she looked as if she were weeping
tears of salt and light.

What made me go to them,
these girls I'd never seen before?
A red string looped around my heart,
the siren call of the camera's shutter
rising and falling?
The need to run
from my parents' most recent battle?

I think
it was all three.

*Hey, mermaids*, I called to them.
*Can I join you?*

**The second girl lowered her camera.**
Her tone blazed with secret fire
as she said,
*Why would we want* that,
*when princes steal our voices?*

*I'm not a prince*, I insisted.

The first girl blinked
the dying light from her eyes.
*You look like one.*

I lifted my arms to show them otherwise,
letting the sunset paint my scars
shell pink.

*A few months ago,*
*a river stole me,* I said.
*The doctors had to crack me open*
*to guide its waters out.*
*Princes get rescued by mermaids*
before *the waves can take them.*
*And I don't expect to be rescued*
*by anybody.*

**The second girl tilted her head,**
some other land's stolen autumn
in her curls.
She held out her camera
like a peace offering.
(Like the hand
she wasn't quite willing to extend.)

*Take our picture,* she dared.
*I want to see*
*how* you *see us*
*and the world.*

In the game of truth or dare,
most boys would refuse
a truth;
it could expose too much of what lies
under our armor.
But none of us can ever refuse
a dare.

(I was no different.)

**In my photos, the girls were a pair of roses**
intertwined,
mermaids set loose from stories
where they were doomed to sea-foam
and heartbreak.
And the distance from one to the other
could be measured
in kisses alone.

My photos always showed them together—
act one of a love story.

The first girl
draped herself around the second,
like the night enfolding Miami
in its arms.
*He should stay*, she whispered.
*He sees us*
*for who we are.*
*The pictures he took prove it,*
*and that's rare in anybody.*
*It's even rarer in a boy.*

I decided to take that
as a compliment.
*I'm Andres, by the way*, I told them.

The second girl
rubbed at her left wrist.
Her own scars were cracks
in her glass-still facade.
*My name's Renee Delgado*, she said.
*Renee means to be born again.*
*And this is Liora Rose.*
*Liora means light.*

Her introduction
was an act of trust.
*Di mi nombre y me romperás*, as the riddle goes:
say my name,
and you will break me.

But none of us had broken the other
with either silence *or* the truth.
(Yet.)

**Renee was the first to notice my guitar,**
that almost-extension of me.
*Why don't you play something*
*for us?* she asked.

I opened my mouth to refuse—
I'd never played outside my bedroom.
But the strings of my guitar
flashed to life on their own.
*Play me, play me!* she cried.

I jumped to my feet and picked up
my guitar.
The music she and I composed
sounded like rhinestones
spilling onto the sand.
I swung my hair
(too long for my father, perfect for me)
and my hips
in time to the new rhyme.

When the outro wound down,
when I'd sunk back to the ground,
Liora stroked my guitar's fretboard, smiling.
*That was like magic—real magic!*
*You and your guitar are special.*
                *I*
                            *can*
                                        *tell.*
*What's her name?*

Was it my voice
or the guitar's that answered her?
Or did we melt together
in the crushing heat?
*Ariel*, I (we) replied.
*Like the little mermaid.*

*Bring Ariel again
tomorrow*, Renee suggested.
*I want to take pictures of you
playing her.*

And that was how the second line
of our-soon-to-be love song
began.

# CHAPTER
## SIX

**Rebirth became a daily occurrence**
when I was with the mermaid girls
at the beach.

Renee in particular was a phoenix,
always transforming
into someone new.

One week, Renee was all vintage:
red lipstick and a broad-brimmed hat,
Audrey Hepburn pulled from a film reel.
The next, she was Wednesday Addams
nearly grown up, tarot cards
in the pockets of her little black dress.

She spread the cards on the sand,
flipping them over

one

        at

            a

                  time.

For Liora, she pulled
the Queen of Cups, the Tower, the Star.
*You're the Queen of Cups*, Renee told her girlfriend.
*Your heart's overflowing*
*with love, like the Queen's chalice.*
*You'll go through changes soon.*
*They may seem frightening at first,*
*but the Tower that falls*
*needs to fall.*
*And your life*
*will be brighter afterward, like the Star.*

For me, she pulled
the Knight of Cups in reverse, Death, the Knight of Cups.
My scars throbbed
as I stared at Death's familiar grin, a reminder
of what I still owed her.
But the last card was responsible
for conjuring Renee's own frown.

*What's wrong?* I asked.

Renee traced the Knight's smooth cheek.
*There's only supposed to be one of these*
*in the deck.*

*When the Knight faces upright,*
*he's a young (and hopeless!) romantic.*
*When he's reversed, the Knight*
*is his own shadow,*
*and his kisses burn*
*like wildfires.*

The constellations
in Liora's eyes glittered as she argued,
*Andres wouldn't hurt anyone!*

Renee swept
the cards into her pocket, her hair over her shoulder.
*Tarot is only a game.*
*I'm sorry if I made it seem*
*like something more.*

I knew a lie
when I heard one;
we liars
recognize our own kind.

But out of sight was (mercifully) out of mind,
and I forgot
the Knight, his shadow, Death's smile
the moment Liora suggested,
*Let's pet the cats that live on the jetty.*
*They could use a little extra love.*
*And if you make a wish*
*on one of their lost whiskers,*
*it's sure to come true.*

**On the jetty, Liora danced on pink toes,**
casting a spell
in the form of a song.
*Your photos*
*will change the world, Renee!* she sang.
*Your music*
*will move every audience to tears, Andres!*
*I just know it!*

*And Liora,*
*you'll be the darling*
*of Juilliard, Broadway, Hollywood,*
*every billboard in every city*, said Renee.

I leaned into their hope,
a sigh
easing from my lips.
I didn't care
if my music ever reached
the ears of monsters, presidents, the men who were both.
I had a sanctuary at the beach,
solace in two girls.
And a sanctuary was all I needed.

**Our homes**
(four in all,
thanks to Mami and Papi's split)
were scattered
like seashells across Miami Beach.

But the three of us
always walked together from the water's edge,
up to the path in Flamingo Park,
where the palm trees stretched their long necks
to eavesdrop
on our conversations.

Twilight was smudged on the edges of the sky
when the park's sprinklers *h i s s e d* to life,
spraying us as we passed.

Liora shrieked a laugh, catching the droplets
in her open palms.
Her smile fae and full of mischief,
she seized Renee's hand—
and then mine.

*Come! On!*
Liora tugged
me and Renee into the sprinklers.
The sweltering evening
turned to cool relief
as the water struck my skin and scars.

Grinning, Renee
chased Liora.
And the reward for catching her girlfriend?
A kiss, of course.
Long and slow, like melting chocolate.

Watching the mermaid girls,
I tried to fight the June heat
rising in me.
But it was too little, too late.
I was already picturing
my lips on Liora's, my mouth on Renee's.
I was already picturing what would be impossible . . .
and wrong.
       (Or so I thought.)

I was grateful
when their kiss ended and the girls
raced on.
Under the jets of water,
our trio arched like rainbows.
And rainbows have always been promises
for a better tomorrow.

As the last of the day
fled into the night, I promised myself
I wouldn't let the hurricanes
my parents blew off their mouths
trail after me.
I wouldn't let Liora and Renee know
my ugly truths.
And when I was with them, I'd try to forget
those truths myself.

I'd be
my *best* self around Renee and Liora;
I'd bring them
torch songs, never tears.
I'd—

**My daisy chain of promises**
slipped through my fingers
as Liora's phone
*howled.*
She stopped spinning and fumbled it
up to her ear, the act clumsy,
when before, she'd been pure grace.

*I wanted to swim a little.*
*It's good for me to exercise*
*different muscles*, Liora mumbled.
Every word
was a shard from a bottle of perfume—
too brittle, too sweet.
*I'll go to the studio*
*for an extra hour tomorrow, to make up*
*the time.*
*Yes. Yes. I'll see you*
*soon.*

The phone went dark and silent.
But Liora's gaze
never left it.

Renee twirled her girlfriend's gold braid
around her finger, a stolen summer moment.
*Ground Control*
*to Major Tom*, she said,
echoing David Bowie, a cosmic faerie prince
gone supernova.
*Come back to earth, Liora.*
*Are you okay?*

Liora's stained glass stillness
cracked.
*Yes!* She laughed, loud
as only sobs should be.
*I'm sorry!*
*But I really should go.*

*Why?*
Renee lifted her chin, checking the sky
for stars.
*It's not even fully dark yet.*

*I need to get up early tomorrow*
*and go to my ballet studio,* Liora said.
*I'll fall*
*out of practice if I don't.*

The trench-deep furrow
appearing between Liora's brows
was a look I'd worn myself.

Was there an ongoing battle
at her house too?
Was she struck by stinging words
whenever she came through her door?
I should have asked;
I should have told her
I knew what it was like to fight in a war
no one can ever win.

But I couldn't shatter
the peace of the evening.
That would have required more courage
than I'd had in months.

I squeezed Liora's hand instead,
hoping
my thoughts (and my love) would seep into her.
*Then we'll see you*
*tomorrow afternoon.*
*Okay?*

*Okay*, said Liora.
She stood on the tips of her toes . . .
and kissed my cheek.
The feel of her lips was light, the brush of a wing
and no more.

But the world bloomed red around me.
Liora, the kiss, the moment. . . .
It felt too good
to be true.

**My dreams expanded as June afternoons**
stretched into July nights and I stopped
thinking in terms of *surviving*
another day or year,
just long enough
to separate myself from my parents,
with kilometers, miles, cities, continents,
a long procession of heartbeats.

My dream became something new:
to take Renee and Liora with me
when I graduated high school.
       (And ran.)
I started an escape fund
at Mami's house and Papi's new one,
saving birthday money, payments for odd jobs,
coins I found on the sidewalk
like the wishes that fell
from Liora's lips.

I didn't tell Renee or Liora about my plan,
my longing for a new life.
       (With them.)
But still, I kept dreaming
of best friends forever.
And, when I dared to, of maybe
       even
more.

# CHAPTER
## SEVEN

**Ever the contrast to me and Liora,**
Renee lived with her parents in an apartment,
      (650 square feet of ivory tile
      on the fourth floor)
where the air was perfumed
with pulled pork, fried plantains, a country lost
to her family.

Her mom and dad
welcomed Liora and me for dinner
with swift kisses on our cheeks,
salsa music rumbling on the speakers.

*Let's play for them!* Ariel cried, jubilant.
How could I refuse?
The notes
her strings hit were tangerine sweet;

Renee's parents added to the rhythm,
clapping, laughing,
heaping plantains on Liora's plate.

*Eat, eat*, they said.
*You are too thin.*

Seven songs later, my fingers aching,
I put Ariel aside to dance
with Renee.
We shimmied and jumped,
a bronzed boy and a ruby-haired girl.

My lips occasionally strayed
too close to Renee's.
She didn't close the distance
from me to her that night; we stayed neutral.
          (Or tried to.)
But can any affair of the heart
          (friendship
          or something deeper)
ever be impartial?

**In Renee's apartment,**
magic went beyond the music.
Cities of candles burned for good health;
a painting of Yemaya,
          the waves breaking
          at her feet in a ballet of swirls and stars,
presided over her ofrendas—
white roses, watermelon, pearl combs.

And in the corner, Death's eyes

     (so empty

     everything could live inside them,

     forests and floods, pointless wars and velvet nights)

rested on me.

She was only a statue; I shouldn't have shivered,

shouldn't have tried to avoid her gaze.

But her plaster smile, cool as her scythe,

seemed too lively.

Had the time come to pay Death

what I owed her?

Renee spun me around

so my back was to Death.

*Ignore the shrines*, Renee told me.

*My parents can be superstitious—*

*and silly.*

*They brought more stories about spirits*

*than suitcases*

*when they came to America.*

        I was more like them

        than I ever wanted to admit.

# CHAPTER
## EIGHT

**On midsummer eve, my first kiss with Liora**
became the third bar of our trio's anthem.

With the ocean surging around us,
Liora leaned in and took my lips
in her own.

(Everything important happens to me
near water;
everything meaningful in my life
takes place
where the current meets the shore.)

**Five facts about Liora's kiss:**
It was soft
as sea-foam and the silk of her ballet slippers.
There was no lead-in; it began
before I could prepare myself.

        (Or push her away.)
It made my heart
open like a music box.
        (Like Liora's already was.)
It asked for more.
        (I wanted to give all of it.)
It wasn't a peck on the cheek;
her lips didn't skim the corner of my mouth.
It was a *real* kiss, toe-curling,
one to be marveled at.
But—

**But I stepped back,**
my eyes moving
from girl-dawn to girl-midnight.
Both were smiling boldly.
*Wait*, I began. *The two of you . . .*

*Are together*, Renee finished,
her lines merging with mine.
*But that doesn't mean*
*we can't also be with you.*

*I like you*, said Liora.
*I like dreaming with you.*
*I like your body.*
*So does Renee.*
*And I think* you *like all those things*
*about me and her too.*

My protest was watered down
by my own doubt.
I flashed a look at Ariel sleeping in her case.
Her silence
left me without a song to help me
rise to the occasion.
*You can't be with more than one person*, I said.
*That's not how love works.*

*Who decided* that? Renee probed.
*Some priest? Some politician?*
*Some executive in a high tower?*
*Someone who probably never loved*
*anyone but themselves.*

*Any rule that limits love*
*doesn't make sense*, Liora added.
*If I like you, if Renee likes you,*
*and if you like the two of us,*
*why can't we be* three?

I thought of Papi,
girl after interchangeable girl
on his arm.
They were like gold bracelets—
shown off for their beauty
but never adored.

Renee and Liora's beauty
had been what drew me to them
on that first sunset,
but not on the forty-four sunsets
after.
I wanted to be a part of their futures.
And wasn't that love?

*We could at least try it*, said Renee.

Liora wrung her hands together.
*Think about it, Andres!*
*The three of us do everything together now!*
*Why not this?*

*Because love*
*is a ballad;*
*it can only hold*
*so many notes, syllables, steps*, I told the girls.

I couldn't tell them
my *real* fear:
whenever there was a third party
in my parents' marriage,
it uprooted what little love the two of them still had
for each other.
What if I did the same
to the mermaid girls?

Renee threaded her fingers in mine,
her long nails coaxing
a shiver of music from my skin.
*We're a circle, not a series of strings*
*about to knot and break.*
*You're already one of us, Andres.*

Resolve, words, melodies all failed me.
But the wind made Ariel's strings sing,
*Love is love.*

What was my reply to the girls and my guitar?
A pair of kisses.
Liora's was sweet as vanilla–ice cream;
Renee's touch sparked like a match.
And me?
I was the Knight of Cups—loved and in love,
my shadow
nowhere to be seen.

**If my father**
had known about Renee and Liora,
he would have congratulated *me*, like they were jeweled birds
ensnared in the net of my charms.

If my mother
had known about Renee and Liora,
she'd rage at me, naming me my father
in miniature,
*boto encantado*, the seducer
from the same river that tried to steal me.

(As if cheating
and being polyamorous were the same.)

And that's why I didn't tell either of my parents
anything at all.
I let secrets
stick to my ribs and the backs of my teeth,
bittersweet as cocoa.

(It was safer that way.)

# CHAPTER
## NINE

**Yesterday, Renee proposed a visit to Vizcaya,**
        a Miami landmark
        I'd never heard of.

*I want to take*
*fairy-tale photos of you two there!*
*It's a modern castle, marooned*
*in the wrong place,* Renee texted
to Liora and I.
*And I want it to be full*
*of all the wrong players—Miami kids*
*instead of princes and princesses*
*in December white.*
*I want to subvert expectations.*

We had nothing to lose
by agreeing.

**I picked Renee up first.**
She whistled at my car—
another guilt gift, this one star silver
to complement Ariel's sea blue.

*You (or your parents)*
*have good taste*, she commented
as we drove north to Liora's house,
fighting the traffic
inch by inch, block by block.

I parked
around the corner from our girlfriend's home.
There was no valley of thorns
separating us from Liora, but there was a wall of hedges
too tall for us to scale.

I'd never set foot in her home before,
but my heart sprung open like a trap
at the sight of it.
The house looked, *felt* too much
like Mami and Papi's.
Lobelia blossoms must have set sail
in the backyard pool;
Liora must have been afraid to tarnish
        the pop art paintings, the floorboards,
        the air itself
with a touch or word.

I couldn't blame her
for not letting us
inside.
But Renee did.
She sighed and sprawled in her seat,
one leg hooked over mine,
while Kurt Cobain
beat a song into our bones.

*I've been with Liora for a year . . .*
*and she's never once*
*invited me over,* Renee mumbled.
*I'd like to meet her mother.*
*If not*
*as her girlfriend, then as her friend.*
*It feels like Liora is hiding me—*
*like I'm something*
*to be ashamed of.*

*Liora isn't ashamed of you,* I assured her.

Renee outlined one of her scars
in time to the music.
       (Even after it ended, the song still played
       under our skins.)
*Maybe.*
*But it's easy to throw someone away*
*when you've never made them*
*a full part of your life.*

My tongue swelled with everything
I wanted to tell Renee.
      (And couldn't.)
She might not understand
how a house like Liora's
wouldn't keep your secrets, unless you were the one
who owned all four walls.

Huffing, Renee stretched backward,
her fingers plucking my soccer ball
off the back seat.
Bouncing it from hand to hand, she said,
*I didn't know you played anything*
*except Ariel.*

I tried for a smile
that would make Papi proud;
I mimicked Mami
at her cinematic best.
*I was on a team at school*
*in Brazil,* I said.
*But that's not important.*

The pause that followed was a wave
about to break over me.

*You hide too many things, Andres—*
*just like Liora*, Renee murmured.
*You tuck your secrets*
*in Ariel's body;*

*Liora wraps hers up*
*in her dance steps.*
*Sometimes I wonder*
*if I know anything about either of you.*

I raised my hands
in false surrender.
If I could have wrapped the clouds around me
and made a white flag from them,
I would have.
*You know*
*the most important things*, I lied.
*And Liora's heart*
*is painted on her sleeve.*
*You know* us, *Renee.*
*So trust us, will you?*

I didn't tell her the truth:
prying open
the treasure box of Liora's heart
was the last thing I wanted to do.

I was afraid
its tangled contents
would look too much
like what was inside *me*.

**Villa Vizcaya was different**
from the rest of Miami; it held a century
in its stones.

James Deering (1859–1925) built the castle
to protect him from northern winters.
Like too many places in this world,
it was created to be
the playground of a white man,
a shrine to his ego.

Sculptures of mermaids
clung to the sides of the mansion, their voices trapped
in their sandstone mouths.
Yemaya's daughters
tried to hold back the tides, the sea, the inevitable
alongside the mangroves
bordering Deering's artificial kingdom.

The gardens
              (the limestone steps flowing from the balconies,
                  the giggling fountains,
                  the marble statues of stoic gods)
were filled with tourists, summer-camp groups,
girls in quinceañera dresses
blooming around them like bouquets.

But despite the crowds,
Vizcaya felt like a private kingdom for our trio,
full of secret roads.
I twirled Liora under the mangroves,
the flash of Renee's camera
changing us both into sunbeams.

*Ground Control*
*to Major Tom!* I sang to the girls.
*You're both roses*
*much kinder*
*than Antoine de Saint-Exupéry's.*

Their laughter was a duet
I could have listened to
all day.

Renee laid out her photos in the deep-purple shade
for Liora and me.
Our shadows mingled briefly
as I swung my head from one girl to the other.
I kissed them both, a hummingbird
caught between two flowers.

But it was my kisses
that lured the other boys
to us.

**The boys were strangers;**
I didn't recognize any of them.
They cackled like the Tietê,
flicking their tongues, spitting insults

(*Slut!*
        *Player!*
                *Perv!*)

at our triad.

The old me
would have launched the insults back, rocket fast.
The new me
put an arm around Liora, defensive.
      (And no more.)

It was Renee
who picked up a chunk of coral,
who catapulted it at the jeering boys,
who shouted,
*Voyeurs! Jerks!*
*Mind your own*
*damn*
*business!*

The boys
dispersed like fog, still snickering.
But Renee's temper didn't—
and it was Liora and me
she turned it on next.
*You two could have said something!* she snapped.
*You both could have helped me!*

Guilt blistered Liora's cheeks
red as a sunburn.
*Renee, please*, she begged.
*Let's not fight; let's just have fun.*

*Liora's right*, I said.
*I don't want to fight with anyone—*
*least of all*
*with either of you.*

My truth
        (simple or cowardly—who could say?)
defused the argument
before it could explode into the open air.

# CHAPTER
## TEN

**There was another truth I carried with me,**
one much darker
than love:
whenever I slept, I only ever dreamed
of drowning.

It was one of those dreams
       (the midnight blue of the river
       four thousand miles away
               crawling
         into
      my lungs)
Renee interrupted with a phone call.

**I AM was too late for anyone to call.**
And that's why
I paddled up from the tides of memory
to settle back in my bed, the last of summer
pressing me into the warm sheets.

A call this late could only mean
*danger.*

I picked up my phone and heard a missive
from a strange universe, urgent
as warnings
always are.
*Something's happened*
*to Liora*, Renee said.

I sat upright, letting the past
       (the darkness
       and the weight of water)
ebb away.
*How do you know?*

I could hear Renee shrug,
her sun-browned shoulders shifting
     up
         and
    down.
*I tried texting her; I tried calling.*
*But she won't pick up.*

*It's 1 AM, I groaned.*
*We spent most of the day*
*at Vizcaya—*
*and Liora had dance class*
*after.*
*She's probably exhausted.*
*But I'll try to reach her too.*
*And in the meantime,*
*don't worry.*
*I'm sure everything*
*is fine.*

**I sent the same text to Liora**
six times:

> *Ground Control*
> *to Major Tom.*

But Liora didn't answer, and dread
built castles in my lungs and belly.
I typed the phrase a seventh time
      —and my phone (finally!) shrieked to life.
I slammed it to my ear, asking,
*Liora?*

*Who is this?*
The question that roared
above the hiss of static and machinery
belonged to a near stranger—
Mrs. Rose, a woman I'd only ever heard
from a distance.

*Who* is *this?* Liora's mother repeated,
her voice the opposite
of her daughter's cloud-soft arias.

*I'm . . .*
        (Her boyfriend.)
*I'm Andres.*
*I'm a friend of Liora's,* I stammered.
*Me and her other friend*
        (our girlfriend)
*were wondering*
*if she was okay.*

Mrs. Rose's voice was pure poison
as she spat,
*My daughter is in the hospital!*
*Don't bother us again!*

                                    The
                                  phone
                              went dead.

**In Miami, the nights are never black;**
they're ballad blue.
Not even a falling star
could catch me as I sped toward Renee's home,
Ariel in the back seat.

*Ground Control*
*to Major Tom*, the ghost of David Bowie
sang on the radio.
I flicked him aside, that phantom
whose song failed to bring me
any closer to Liora.

But I wasn't sure what *would*.

Death had demanded something I loved
in exchange
for her miracle:
a future whose hues
came in more than poppy-colored rage.

But was Liora's future
the price I'd paid for my own?

**Renee stood in the doorway of her building,**
her Polaroid camera
       (blue as ojo malo, the evil eye
       meant to ward off the wicked)
dangling from her neck, purple oleander raining down
at her feet.

The flowers
should have made her look like royalty.
But in Brazil,
purple isn't the color of kings and queens.
In Brazil,
purple is the color of grief.

I opened the car door; Renee leaped inside.
And we resumed the conversation
we'd begun
through the wires of our thoughts alone.

*Liora's mother didn't tell me*
*which hospital she's in—*
*or why*, I said.
*She didn't tell me*
*anything.*

But why would she?
To Mrs. Rose,
Renee and I were names (without faces)
flashing on the forever-cracked screen
of Liora's phone.
Her bond with our girlfriend
was forged in blood;
our claim was just a string of kisses
she knew nothing about.

The circles under Renee's eyes
were nearly black;
they held the light hostage.
*Liora's at Mount Sinai Hospital.*
*I can feel her there*
*like a weight.*
*Come on.*
*We don't have much time.*

# CHAPTER
## ELEVEN

**The two of us wove like smoke**
through the labyrinth of the hospital,
searching each floor
for a heartbeat that could play a refrain
with our own.

We stayed quiet, avoiding
the moon-serene doctors, the soon-to-be-mourners.
Only Ariel spoke, her melody
insistent.
*This way, this way, this way*, she chanted.

So I followed her lead, and Renee
followed mine.

Only my seventh text had been answered,
so how could I be shocked
when we found Liora on the seventh floor?

The door to her room hung open.
Her chart swung from it, bleeding words
that tried to draw blood from *me*:

*Car accident.*
*Severe head trauma.*
*Nonresponsive.*
*Coma.*

**Love was**
everlasting,
evermore.

But forever was no more.

Liora had been emptied of her song;
she lay in the hospital bed,
clothed in a saint's whites,
her body a heap of bones
and fragile breaths.
A plastic jungle
burst out of her hands, her nose, her belly—
places where Renee and I
had both planted kisses.

Death wasn't at Liora's bedside,
poised to cut the thread of her life.
But as I wavered on the threshold,
I felt the end of all things beside me
just the same.

**Renee and I became a storm surge;**
we spilled
into the room—
and a hand
   shot
      out
to bar our way
more effectively than any seawall.

*What*
   *are you*
     *doing here?*
The woman in our path, Mrs. Rose,
was a glacier
in the wrong latitude.
Each of her edges was pale, thin, jagged.
Tears melted down her face,
created by the Miami heat
and the ghost orchid of a girl
in the bed.

Renee forced herself
farther into the room, the unstoppable force
to this woman's unmovable object.
*Andres and I*
*are Liora's friends*, she said.
*We knew she was here.*
*We need to—*

The woman pointed to the door,
her thin fingers
striking the air.
But I think she would have preferred
to strike *us*.

*Get out!* Mrs. Rose howled.
*This is family business!*
*The two of you*
*aren't welcome here!*
*Go home*
            *and stay away*
*from my daughter!*

I met her
snarl for snarl, step for step.
*I'm*
            *not*
                        *leaving!*
*I'm*
            *not*
                        *abandoning*
*Liora!*

I reached out for Liora;
I reached out to seize Mrs. Rose's silk blouse.
But it was Renee who reached *me* first.
She grabbed my wrist, hauling me
from Liora's coffin of a room.

*What are you doing?*
I shouted, scrambling for the empty shell
Liora had become.
*We can't just go!*

Renee's grip tightened, countering
my desperation with quiet strength.
*We can't do anything for Liora*
*here.*
*And fighting with her mother*
*won't help her at all.*

The inferno in me
retreated,
replaced by shame just as hot.
I had reverted
to the Andres of Brazil,
the boy who became a lightning strike
whenever he was confronted.

I ground
my heels into the floor, rooting myself
in the now.
I needed to be everything
I bargained with Death for.
(Especially
if Liora was the price for my new self.)

*What*
*are we going to do?* I asked softly.

Renee bit her cherry-glossed lip.
*You have to come with me.*
*I . . .*
> *I may.*
>> *I may have a plan.*

# CHAPTER
## TWELVE

**Eager for the hospital to fade from view,**
I drove far too fast
out of Mount Sinai's parking lot,
and onto the Julia Tuttle Causeway.

The bridge was one of three ways
off Miami Beach,
stretching python long between the island
and the mainland.
We were protected from the world here;
we were trapped far from it.
We were both things at once,
running in shades of gray, like the strange city
I'd seen from the borders
of Death's country.

Renee wouldn't look at me
as she tore her next words out of her throat,
one syllable
at a time.
*Andres, listen.*
*I lied*
*about the tarot cards.*
*They're not a game; they never were.*
*And reading them*
*isn't the only magic I can do.*

I remembered Mami and Papi's curses,
how they'd failed to stick.
Yet with her cards, Renee had read *me*
like I was a poem she'd already memorized;
she'd even seen the shadow
I'd been liberated from.

But Liora's glass-still form
needed a different sort of miracle.

*We can't pull Liora out of a coma*
*with the strike of a match*
*or a candle dressed in rose water*, I argued.
*A head injury isn't a cyclone*
*you can send north*
*by offering rum to a god.*
*Death is one storm*
*you can't pray away.*

*No*, Renee admitted, *you can't.*
*But you and I*
*might be able to find Liora's spirit*
*and guide her back*
*to her body.*
            *If we go to the underworld,*
*we could bring Liora* home.
*It's called* soul retrieval.
*My grandmother*
*taught me how to do it*
*when she was still alive.*


**I slammed**

my foot on the brakes, pitching us
both forward.
But really, I had been thrown
back into the past.


The tempo of my breath sped up,
trying to assert
my place among the living.
Because if I returned to the underworld,
my shadow would be waiting for me . . .
and whoever came with me.
And what would happen if it found Renee and me
before we found Liora?

I couldn't risk that happening;
I couldn't risk putting either of my girlfriends
in reach of a jaguar's claws—
or a prince's kiss.
I couldn't risk them realizing
the truth about me.


*I won't leave Liora*
*in the dark*, Renee pressed.
*If I have to,*
*I'll go to the underworld myself;*
*Dante and Odysseus, Aeneas and Inanna*
*all descended alone.*
*But I could use some company.*
*I could use a hand*
*to hold.*
*I could use—*


*Renee, enough!* I shouted,
abrupt
as my sudden stop.
*That kind of magic*
*is too dangerous.*
*We'll end up like Liora—*
*lost, with no road home.*

**Renee turned her gaze, cold as November,**
on me.
*What do you think* real *magic is?*
*It's not a toy*
*dispensed by a vending machine,*
*not a firecracker*
*you can blow out like a birthday candle*
*when its spark gets too bold.*

*Magic is*
*fire in your blood like a fever.*
*Magic is*
*the black door to worlds between worlds.*
*Magic is*
*the path of pins, the path of needles.*

*Magic isn't*
fuck around.
*Magic is*
find out.

*But magic is worth doing*
*for love.*
*Or are all your songs and kisses*
*just hollow promises, Andres?*

**My girlfriend and I stared each other down.**
Our edges usually fit together
so neatly;
they didn't dig into the soft and tender places
inside me.

But loss
could make a knife of anyone.

My eyes drifted
out to sea as I whispered,
*Renee, I'm sorry.*
*But I can't.*

I felt the purple veil of hurt
over Renee's heart.
But she didn't
        (she *couldn't*)
understand how much I already knew
about magic . . .
or how much I wished
I *didn't*.

*Coward,* Renee hissed.
*You*
        *damn*
            *coward.*

**Silence is a heavy burden to carry,**
especially with someone you love.
And it was a burden that crushed Renee and me
as I took her home.

She fled my car
the moment
I cut the engine.

I wanted to tell Renee,
*Good luck.*
I wanted to tell her,
*I'm sorry.*
I wanted to tell her,
*I love you and Liora*
*both.*

She slammed the door
before I could decide
what to say.

Loneliness settled in my belly, stinging
like salt water.
Without Renee, without Liora,
I was alone
in a way I hadn't been since moving
to Miami.
I had only my memories to keep me
company.

And it was memory that engulfed me
as I tore through the neon-splattered streets.

# CHAPTER
## THIRTEEN

**Once (and only once) did I break**
my promise to be the best of who I was
when I was with my girlfriends.

Only once did I let my pain
sneak over the borderlands
between the three of us.

Renee never saw that pain . . .
but Liora did.

**The transition from Mami's house to Papi's**
was never peaceful.
I was a human shield,
shoved out of one car or the other,
then deposited
at the door of the so-called enemy.

But that evening
was the worst one so far.
My shoulders curled to shield myself,
I raced
into Papi's house to the thunder
of his and Mami's argument.

> (*You're always late!*
> *You never listen!*
> *You set a bad example!*
> *If you don't behave better, our son—*
> *—will become just like you!*)

Usually, I was able to stay
on the outskirts of their tragedy,
protected by doors, the music sparkling on Ariel's strings,
the steady ring of text messages sent and received.
But that night, too many of their remarks
were aimed at me.

And as my parents
continued to batter each other in my name,
my head buzzed
with one thought alone:
I needed
        to
                get
                        OUT.

I dropped my backpack
      (full of sheet music, an old soccer uniform,
      a small life made even smaller)
onto my bed.
I only took my wallet and Ariel;
like any prisoner
whose sentence had spanned an entire lifetime,
I knew not to carry much.

I climbed out the window
and dropped into the azaleas
breaking in golden waves
at the foundations of Papi's house.
      And then

           I

                    ran.

Did Mami and Papi
realize I'd left them?
No.
Their grudges took up more space
in their houses and their lives
than I ever dared to.

**I drifted along the streets of Miami Beach,**
struggling to tame my fox-quick heartbeat.

I had no destination in mind, no endgame;
I found myself
at Liora's ballet studio anyway.

Even wanderers have to return home.
(Eventually.)
And what's a home if not somewhere
                (some*one*)
you can belong to?

**I perched on the back of a bench,**
more blackbird than boy
and watched Liora dance on a cloud of music.
She mapped out
a fairy tale with the flutter of a hand,
the point of a toe, the serenity of her smile.

*Serenade her!*
*Romeo to Juliet,*
*lover to beloved,* Ariel suggested,
her blue body shining with the music
and the message
she longed to send into the world.
*Let her know how much*
*Liora means to you.*

But my hands refused to move.
Pain had turned me to silence and stone.

**The day came to a gentle close.**
One by one,
the other ballerinas left the studio,
their farewells clinging to the sticky air
long after they'd gone.

It was Liora
who stayed behind, who glided over to me.
She skimmed
her hands through my hair, her touch feather soft.
*Andres,*
*what are you doing here?* she asked.
*What's wrong?*

My body shuddered
like earthquake country.
I wanted to strike
the bench, the palm tree next to it, Ariel's fretboard.
But I couldn't do that to my guitar—
or to Liora.

(I couldn't let the shadow I'd cut out
back *in*.)

So I wrestled
the simplest version of the story
free.
*My parents*
*won't stop bringing their rage, their pain*
*home to me!*
*And it's getting harder and harder*
*to shake off.*

Liora rested her cheek against mine.
*Their fight isn't yours,* she whispered.
*Don't keep it locked up*
*inside you.*

I couldn't go to war
with Mami and Papi or boys on the street.
        (Anymore.)
But l could easily go to war
with *myself.*

Fists trembling, l told Liora,
*I hate them sometimes!*
*I know I shouldn't;*
*I should love them, listen to them*
*without question.*
*But I can't stand what they do to each other,*
*how watching them makes me feel.*
*And I can't stay*
*in either of those houses.*
                *I*
                        *just*
                                *can't.*

Liora worried
her pink lip with her teeth.
It made her look like the little girl
I'd never known her as, unsure of her footing
in the world.
*I wish*
*I could tuck you into a corner*
*of my house, underneath my blankets.*
*I wish*
*you could come home with me.*
*But my mom. . . .*

*I understand*, I told her.
And I did.

Liora could have hugged me
one last time and returned to her life,
her dance lessons, her mother's wishes.
(Whatever they were.)
But she didn't.

My girlfriend folded me
up in her arms, in the feeling of *home*.
*When you go back to your parents*
            *(because you* need *to go back),*
*call me*, said Liora.
*We can talk and talk and talk—*
*until you fall asleep,*
*if that's what you need.*
*I can even sing,*
*if you think it would help.*

*I can't let you*
*waste your time like that*, I said.

Liora kissed my forehead.
Her lipstick
left the ghost of a rose behind.
*It's not a waste of time*
*to help someone you love.*

**That night, I listened to Liora's song,**
my phone cradled against my cheek.
My girlfriend was with me—
in spirit, if nothing else.

As I sank into sleep,
Liora's iridescent voice
became a blue morpho butterfly, beating back
the hurricanes in my life.

Her music promised
our shared dreams might come true.

Can they, still?

Only if I set my fear aside;
only if I plunge back into the dark;
only if I save Liora—
the way she saved me.

# CHAPTER
## FOURTEEN

**3 AM has crept up on me and I've arrived**
at Liora's house
almost by accident.

Without her to animate it, it looms
too large, too empty in the night that will soon fade
to daybreak.

I scratch away the tears
now scarring my cheeks.
They taste like stale anger, the Tietê River,
the underworld.
        (And what I happily lost there.)
They taste like my last kiss with Liora.

Rescuing my girlfriend may cost me
everything
I am.

But isn't love worth any price?
And don't I owe it to Liora
to take back
what I've done to her?

My body tries to resist
any action
doomed to drag my soul out of it.
It takes me three tries to find Renee's number
on my phone;
it takes another three to tame my hands
long enough to call.

She picks up
after only one ring.

Holding tight to the memory of Liora's song,
I say to Renee,
*I've changed my mind.*
*I'm coming with you*
*to the underworld.*
*Tell me everything*
*you know.*

I hear Renee's smile through the wires,
ruthless, fearless . . .
but not hopeless.
*I'd hoped you'll call.*

**The flame-struck girl, my brighter side of midnight,**
lowers her voice.
*My grandmother told me*
*the underworld*
*is a City.*

*It's a shadow*
*of all the cities on earth*
*that ever were and ever will be.*
*But nothing sparkles in that place.*
*Sorrow stole the stars above it,*
*and the streets are paved with tears.*

*The only songs anybody can play*
*are written by the dead.*
*The spirits shake their hips*
*to the likes of Bowie, Prince, Judy Garland.*

*The living have different names for the City.*
*Hel, Dis, Pandemonium,*
*Xibalba, Gehenna, Irkalla.*
*We think of the grief there*
*as divine punishment, fire and brimstone—*
*so we call it* Hell
*instead of* a haunting.

*But in the City,*
*the dead haunt* themselves.
*They cling to lives*
*already spent like coins and candles;*
*they mourn*
*the loss of who they were*
*and who they'll never be now.*

I ask,
*Wouldn't the only door*
*to a place like that*
*be death?*
(It was for me, the last time.)

*There's another road there*, Renee insists.
*Old places are* thin *places,*
*places where worlds meet*
*like the walls of a house,*
*where you can feel a ghost's hand*
                *creeping into yours*
*and not become one of them.*
*To cross over, to go* under,
*we have look beyond*
*the glass condos, the flooded streets,*
*the still waters of Miami.*
*We have to look*
*to the past.*

*So Andres,*
　　　　*are you*
*still*
　　　　*with*
*me?*

My heart doesn't allow me a choice.
(It never does.)
*I'll pick you up*
*in fifteen minutes.*

# CANTO II
## SO BELOW

# CHAPTER
## FIFTEEN

**We drive on US-1, Miami's electrified spine.**
Away from the endless galas of South Beach,
the roads are stone-still;
there's no one awake to question
why me and Renee are out so late;
we have the city to ourselves.

But with every mile we travel,
my love-swollen heart
sinks
a little lower . . .
and my reunion with my shadow
feels more and more inevitable.

*Tell me where I'm going*, I say to Renee.
*Where can we find*
*old and hallowed ground*
*in a city this new?*

Renee rolls down her window,
letting the night air
flow into her outstretched hand.
The other thumbs her camera's shutter.

      (If she's trying to learn how to capture the darkness,

        she should have come to me first.)

*The oldest magic here*
*is in the Everglades.*
*But it isn't ours;*
*it belongs to the Seminole Tribe.*
*We already took their land;*
*we can't steal their magic too.*
*We'll go back*
*to Vizcaya.*
*It's the oldest place in Miami*
*I can think of.*

**I leave my car**
under the arms of a magnolia tree
a few blocks from Vizcaya,
and feed the meter all the money I have—
as if it will do any good.

A journey to the underworld
could take a hundred years;
we could return to find Yemaya governing Miami
with her tides.
A journey to the underworld
could take ten minutes;
we could return, kids through the magic wardrobe,
with hours left to spare.

Renee has already started toward the villa,
but I waver, my keys in hand.
It's Ariel
who makes me hesitate.
She calls to me, her would-be songs
straining to meet my fingertips.

> (*Take me with you!* she begs.
> *I can help.*)

In the end, it's a glimpse of Renee's camera
                (its wide eye fixed on the future)
that makes me give in to Ariel's pleas.

A guitar and a camera
aren't practical tools to bring
on our descent.
But going unarmed
doesn't feel right either.
We need
whatever makes us powerful.

# CHAPTER
## SIXTEEN

**Vizcaya's pale stucco walls aren't high.**
       (For all five feet,
          nine inches of me, that is.)
I hoist myself to the top,
Ariel bobbing at my side, and lean down,
taking Renee by the waist.
I pull her easily
         up
and
         over the wall,
where the ferns shelter us
from streetlamps and prying eyes.

At this hour, we're alone
in the dim gardens
except for the pack of security officers
prowling the grounds.

Their eyes are waxing moons
on the verge of closing;
their guns dangle
lazily from their belts.
We sneak past them, like we're more spirit
than skin already.

**Memory hunts me**
the way guards don't bother to.
How can it not, when the last time we came here,
we were with Liora?

Bottling my tears
at the back of my throat, I can't help wishing
         (on satellites and airplanes)
we had something of Liora's here with us—
a lock of hair, her ballet slippers,
seven bars from the song she was writing
in the back of her day planner.

I dare to ask Renee,
*Do you remember*
*the pink dress Liora wore*
*when you took our photos here?*
*Do you remember*
*how we each snuck a kiss with her*
*behind a mangrove tree?*

Renee's face crumples and she looks away—
from me and the memory.
*Of course I do; a day*
*isn't a lifetime.*
*But it's better*
*not to play that game.*
*Liora isn't gone;*
*we don't need to burn up our time*
*remembering someone*
*who will be back home soon.*

Is Renee lecturing me . . .
or reassuring *herself*?
It must be a bit of both.

**In the very heart of the garden,**
we stop
at the largest fountain, its waters as fickle and wild
as I used to be.

Renee places:

      seven squares of chocolate,

      seven red rose petals,

      seven unlit cigarettes
on the fountain's coral rim.
*They're ofrendas*
*for Death*, she explains.
*So we won't arrive in her lands*
*as unwanted guests.*

Renee steps
around her offerings and into the fountain.
I take her hand and follow,
as I always do.

(And hope I always will.)

My girlfriend's instructions
are satin soft, almost hesitant.
*If you're sure about this,*
*lie down*
*and hold your breath.*

*And make a wish?* I half joke.

But Renee's solemn as she says,
*It might not hurt.*
*There could be shooting stars*
*listening even now.*

I chuckle.
(After all,
aren't we supposed to laugh in graveyards?)
*That sounds like something*
*Liora would have said.*

Renee kisses my cheek.
*And she'll say it again—*
*if we're both brave.*
*Now think about Liora.*
*Focus on her.*

*Think about what she'd look like*
        *(a living string*
        *of fairy lights)*
*in a place where nothing else*
*gleams.*
*And let that image guide you*
*down.*

Panic unravels
the steady rhythm of my heart, turning it to a cry
I have to swallow.
I've dreamed of drowning
for months.
But I never thought I'd have to drown
in the waking world again.

*Renee is a mermaid,* Ariel reminds me
as I cradle her against my chest.
*You may not be a prince*
        *(anymore),*
*but she won't leave you*
*to the mercy of the water.*

Trusting Renee and the music,
I lie back in the fountain.
My girlfriend submerges me—a strange baptism,
hell-bent instead of heaven-sent.
But I traveled to Death's golden lands
this way before, didn't I?
So, of course, I'd take the same road
twice.

I let myself
> sink.

I let the familiar darkness
> wrap me in its cool embrace.

I let go of the world
> above and enter the world—

# CHAPTER
## SEVENTEEN

**Below, where I hear the Tietê River**
mocking me and my return.
*Welcome back*, it cackles.
*For the second*
         *(and maybe, the last)*
*time.*

Beating back the dark,
I fight to the surface,
willing the air to reenter my throbbing lungs.
Clawing at my stinging eyes,
I shove my hair from my face
and look up.

A slice of me
         (more rational
         than any musician has the right to be)

expects the world to be unchanged,
for me to emerge dripping
and just as lost as before.

But I'm not in the living Vizcaya
on Planet Earth.
I'm back in the land
where the constellations have abandoned the sky.

               I'm back in the world of the dead.

**The country of endings hasn't dimmed Renee's fire.**
She's stone steady
as she climbs out of the fountain,
shaking our journey, beads of water, all her doubts
aside.

I should be relieved to have a companion,
but I battle a grimace
as Renee helps me to my feet,
my hands crackling with
        a sudden
              searing
                 *ache.*
I must have fallen
too far, too fast and cut myself
on the jagged edges where one world
meets with the next.

But when I open my fists,
there are no wounds on them, no bruises I can wear
like medals.
There are shadows
caked in my palms, thick as river silt.
And they are shaped
like black stars.

I thought I'd have more time
before *any* fragment of my shadow
discovered me here.
But time is something the underworld
*lacks*.

I cram my hands into my pockets, grateful
Renee didn't notice the secrets
penned on my skin.

**The downside version of Vizcaya**
is home to no one but the court of night.

Spiders crushed by shoes
              (their limbs akimbo)
and possums struck by cars
              (their jaws twisted)
hide in dead jasmine flowers,
withered evening primroses,
fields of dune grass plowed under.

The broken animals
trundle past Renee and I;
the crumbling flowers
try to entice us with their phantom perfume.
I pull back,
not wanting their bony limbs and waxy leaves
to touch me.

> (I can't risk their shadows
> calling to my own.)

Renee takes my hand a second time.

> (I refuse to flinch;
> the pain in my palms is a phantom
> I want to let go of.)

*Don't tell me*
*you're afraid of spiders,* she teases.

*Not of them,* I mutter.
*Just of things in the dark.*
(Things like my shadow.)

My girlfriend pulls me closer.

> (If I were still a prince,
> she could draw me like a knife
> and hack through
> this forever night.)

*Then don't go too far;*
*I don't want to lose you.*

> I don't miss how her gaze
> rests on the space
> where Liora should be.

**Holding tight to our quest and each other,**
we walk past the rippling fountains.
Behind us
is Death's true country; it glows on the horizon
in a hundred hues
conjured by souls and roses.

Renee traces a map in the air.
*I think that's where*
*the dead are* supposed *to go*
*when they're finished*
*on earth.*
*It's beautiful, in a way.*

I make my expression moonstruck, awestruck,
like I've never wandered
to this corner of the universe,
like I've never seen
Death's sugar-white smile.
*It* is *beautiful*, I agree.
*But I don't think*
*it's where we need to go.*

*No*, Renee sighs.
*It isn't.*

We continue
through the downside garden till we arrive
at a wall
of almost-familiar banyan trees,
their roots drinking greedily from barren soil.
But this time,
there's no river bringing colors
      (parakeet green and butter yellow)
to their graying leaves.
All that's left of those waters
is a dry gutter
snaking into the depths of the woods,
where the trees are stark and black.


Renee and I may be lovers
in the era of global warming,
but magic
outlives both droughts and rising seas.
So how can an entire river
      (enchanted, eternal)
vanish in six
      short
            months?
I bite my tongue
before I can ask.
Questioning the river's disappearance
would reveal too much.

If Renee knew
who I was before,
if she knew
Liora might be trapped here
because of *me*,
her love would evaporate
along with the river
and the last days of our summer.

**Beyond the banyans**
and the dark forest barring out path
is a City
        (proper noun status deserved)
I remember too well.

It's as far from Miami as any city can be.
It has no iridescent lights
drenching its palm trees and glass palaces
in a deluge of electric blue and pink.
What I see instead are
the broken columns of Roman amphitheaters,
the brutalist towers of Warsaw,
the opaque skyscrapers of New York,
all garbed in mist.
The City's architects
aren't just a handful of men;
they must be the entire human race.

*The City*
*looks so far from here*, I murmur.
*And I can barely see inside this forest.*
*How do we find our way across it?*

Renee sweeps away a moth,
its wings melted by rain.
*My grandmother believed*
*everyone has a spirit that follows them*
*throughout their lives.*
*They whisper warnings to us in our dreams,*
*console us with their warmth,*
*shield us from the evil eye.*

*The Norse called them* fylgja;
*we might call them* familiars.
*But they only become visible to us*
*in our final hours . . .*
*or here*
*in the underworld,*
*where our deaths are closer*
*than ever.*
*One of those spirits*
*should be able to guide us*
*into the woods and up to the gates*
*of the City.*

A spirit?
I imagine an angel
        (*San Miguel Arcángel,*
        *defiéndenos en la batalla.*
        *Sé nuestro amparo . . .* )
or a demon descending on us,
accompanied by a celestial choir
or the shriek of damned souls.
But the only song I hear
is the quiet melody of the after hours.

*I don't see*
*anyone or anything here*
*that can help us,* I say.

And that's when the banyan trees
stir.

I dart
in front of Renee to be her shield;
she slips
under my arm to be mine.
        (We're in an equal partnership
        of stubbornness.)

# CHAPTER
## EIGHTEEN

**The boughs of the banyans retreat, and I prepare**
for a wolf, a lion, a leopard.
It's what Dante found when he lost *himself*
in woods like these,
at the very outskirts of the underworld.

        (On the road to Hell
        itself.)

But what struts
from the banyan labyrinth to greet us
is a *peacock*, a Fabergé egg of a bird
in royal blues and greens.
It hops from root to root, spreading its tail feathers
in welcome.

*I am here*
*for you*, the peacock announces,
bowing his plumed head to Renee.
The bird isn't speaking
English or Spanish, Portuguese or French Creole;
his mother tongue
is a series of chirps and hisses.
Yet I can understand him—
and Renee must too.

*For me?* she asks, bewildered.

*I chose to follow you when you were born*
*because I knew*
*your soul was like mine*, the peacock replies.
*We both find beauty*
*where others cannot;*
*We are both reborn*
*as something better*
*each time we show our whirlwind of colors*
*and let the world see* all *of us.*

Renee's fingers circle her camera's eye,
restless and uncertain.
*That doesn't sound*
*anything like me.*

*That's how I see you*, I say.
*And how Liora does too.*

(Why can't we ever see *ourselves*
as we are?
Why we do always need
a photo, a film reel,
another person
to show the truth of us?)

**Another shape crawls**
through the web of banyan trees.
But the animal that stalks to *my* side
is no bird.
It's the witching hour come to life,
death on dark paws:
a black jaguar.

I want to banish her
before I can meet her moonstone eyes.
But the only place I've been
where black jaguars grow like rot and hemlock
is Brazil.

The jaguar
twines herself around me, a garrote.
She stinks of dead flowers,
the slow burn of anger.
*And I am here*, she says,
*for* you, *Andres*.

I growl at her.

(Two can play this game.)

*I don't trust anything*
*living in the shadows;*
*I don't trust anything*
*that tries to stay hidden.*

The black jaguar lowers her head
and her voice.

> (It scrapes my ears and the dusty earth
> whose river was taken
> before its time.)

*Then you don't trust*
yourself.

**Renee's eyes are firefly fast**
as they dart from me to the jaguar.
*I expected*
*different spirits,* she tells me,
careful as she rarely is.

I'm quick to say,
*The jaguar must have mistaken me*
*for another boy.*
A lie can be an omission;
it can also be part truth.
This jaguar
walked alongside the boy
I *was,*
not the boy
I was remade into.

*There are no mistakes*
*in the underworld.*
*There is only truth*, the peacock replies.
*You want to go to the City, yes?*
*We can take you there.*

*Even with you leading us, we'll stumble*
*in this darkness*, I point out.
*Can you give us*
*a light of our own?*

The peacock swings his head.
*This place is mind*
*over matter.*
*If you think bright thoughts,*
*you will find the light you need*
*in yourself*
*or someone precious to you.*

What makes a boy like me
(marked with black stars)
soar?
My thoughts have rarely shone . . .
but I want to believe
my music does.

I cradle Ariel's neck,
my fingers blurring on her silver strings
as I start to play.

I think of fireworks on New Year's Eve,
August hanging in a fiery cloud
above our city.
I think of fevers breaking, Renee crafting fairy-tale photos.
I think of Liora waking, Lady Lazarus
happy to have returned.
I think of a home for our triad, a garden protecting us
with both thorns and petals.

I think of *hope*.

Light gathers—
not at *my* fingertips, but at Renee's,
in jack-o'-lantern bursts of orange and white.
She nods her thanks
and places her bright hands
on the eye of her camera—
her sword and shield, like Ariel is mine.

Renee clicks
the shutter button, and light
         (hers and mine combined)
erupts from the lens,
blazing through
the twilight of the woods.

A photograph flutters into my hands.
It's a picture of Liora dancing . . . and she moves
like she's dancing still.

It's one of my *memories*, and somehow,
it's come to life.

This shouldn't be possible.
But: mind over matter.
What pours from our heads
paints itself on the photo paper here.

# CHAPTER
## NINETEEN

**We, guides and questers, leave the safety of the garden**
   (as everyone has to, all the way back
   to Adam and Eve)
and begin our journey into the woods.

The animals pad ahead,
their eyes far keener than ours
in this night
without borders or boundaries.
I hold the photo memory of Liora,
a lantern for Renee and me.

There's no road here
   (yellow brick or otherwise),
only the empty riverbed,
a scar
in the very skin of the universe.

Renee drops to one knee, pushing her fingers
into the cracked earth.
*Was there a river here?* she asks the animals.
*Or a sea?*

The peacock scratches at the dust.
*The river's name was* Lethe—
*the river of forgetfulness,*
*the river of unmindfulness.*
*But the dead of the City drank from it*
*till*

         *every*

                *last*

                        *drop*

*was gone.*
*They wanted to forget*
*their lives, their pain, their losses.*
*And the river water allowed them*
*to do just that.*

*Until it didn't,* I mutter.
*Peace is usually temporary.*
        (Every house I've ever been in
        has taught me *that*.)

Renee flips her hair over one shoulder,
a red cloak.
*Oblivion*, she declares, *is overrated anyway.*

**The trees in this strange forest**
rise from soil as black as my hair.
It should be rich; it should give them strength.
But this forest is made of
charred alders and birches,
evergreens hollowed out by insects,
weeping willows felled by floods,
rotten oaks cradling the remains of tree houses,
sycamores with ancient love letters
carved on their trunks.

Every tree here is wounded
from wildfires, diseases, the axes of loggers.
Each tree here is *dead*.

*I guess it's not only human souls*
*that arrive in the underworld*
*after they die*, muses Renee.
Everything *dies, one way*
*or the other.*

We pass a lonely palm tree, broken in two—
like us.
Renee lingers at its deathbed
       (as I wanted to linger
         at Liora's side in her hospital room),
tracing the initials
etched on its side.
*RR*, squared.

*I know this tree; I know these names*, Renee says.
*My uncle Roberto*
*used to shimmy up it*
*and toss down coconuts for me.*
*He'd split them with a machete*
*and toast to me and my future*
*over sips of coconut water.*
*He told me stories too—*
*about the river woman*
*weeping for her drowned children,*
*and the Yara lights—*
*the golden orbs in the sugarcane fields*
*that coax travelers off the path*
*and into their hungry arms.*

I'm cat curious about Renee's childhood—
but I cling to kindness first,
as Ariel reminds me
with the twang of a major seventh chord:
B, D sharp, F sharp, B.

*You never told me this before*, I say gently.
*Just like you never told me*
*about your grandmother's magic.*

There's a distance in Renee's eyes
I can't cross.
She belongs to the past, not the present.

*The palm tree fell in a hurricane.*
*And my uncle died of cancer*
*not long after*, she says,
as if I'd never spoken.
*I was little—six, maybe seven.*
*I hadn't thought about them*
*in years.*
*So maybe this is the country of memory too—*
*and*

       *not*

          *just death.*


**Like so much of this forest, I feel like I'm burning.**
As Renee and I
leave the palm tree and her history,
I sneak a glance at my hands.


The shadows have spread
across head, fortune, life lines.
They deepen and darken by the second.
It's as if all the songs
I can't bring myself to write
       (the ballads to love gone sour,
         the bitter anthems to my childhood)
are leaking out of me, one bar of music
at a time.


I push my hands back in my pockets,
feigning a chill.

(Of course the kingdom of the dead
would be corpse cold.)

**In this wood of echoes and grand finales,**
other people begin to appear.
They wear hospital gowns,
the green uniforms of armies
I've only ever seen
on the news,
street clothes streaked with muck.

These are bent with exhaustion,
the recollection of having a body
weighed down by injury and pain.
They turn slowly—
first to the City, then to the horizon,
where Death's own garden
spreads like the red tide of a new day
they'll never see.

*Who are all these people?* I ask my jaguar.
        (Little as I want to speak to *her*.)
*What are they doing here?*

Her answer is the growl of thunder.
*They are making their final choice:*
*to accept their deaths*
*or deny them as best they can*
*by traveling to the City.*
*The City is an attempt at life—*
*one that never quite succeeds.*

*But it tempts these displaced souls*
               *(like apples, pomegranates, pieces of silver)*
*with its false promises.*
*It's closer to what they lost*
*than what lies ahead.*

I squeeze Renee's hand,
my heart drumming with unexpected hope.
*Maybe Liora is here,*
*somewhere in these woods!*
*You said it yourself,*
*she's* between *life and death.*

Renee pivots, creating a new gutter
beside the riverbed.
*It's possible!*
*I'll go right; you go left.*
*If we don't find Liora, we'll meet again*
*at my uncle's palm tree.*

# CHAPTER
## TWENTY

**We part—not with a kiss, but with a nod.**
A kiss feels too final,
a goodbye that might last
well past the end of the night.

Renee's peacock flies after her,
his kaleidoscope of feathers
a torch lighting her way,
as the picture of Liora
lights mine.
They're a parade, while my jaguar and I
are an unpleasant afterthought.

How can I be who I want
when a sliver of my shadow walks beside me?

*You look like you're sinking
in thought*, the jaguar comments.

*I didn't ask for your opinion*
*on anything,* I snap,
making her sharpness my own.

      (Or have I called my old sharpness
      *back* to me?)

The jaguar doesn't shrink away.
*Denying me*
      *(and your history)*
*won't save* you *from the darkness,*
*inside you or out.*
*And it won't save Liora.*
*Trust me—*
*I've been beside you*
*your whole life.*

I refuse to look at my guide
as I say,
*I don't need* you *to help me*
*save her either.*

*Ah, but you do.*
*To rescue Liora,*
*you need every part of yourself—*
*and that includes your wounds.*
The jaguar's words trap me
like the bars of the cage
she'll never allow herself to be caught in.

*That is, if you're capable of making those wounds*
*into wisdom.*
*Your parents*
*turned their own into weapons,*
*used them*
*to hack at the wrong people.*
*They could have beaten their swords*
*into plows;*
*they could have taught you not to make*
*their mistakes.*
*Instead, they gave you*
*barbed wire edges.*

*Don't talk about that!* I warn,
as if I have anything to threaten
the jaguar with.

> (I can't ask Death to cut away
> a part of me for the second time
> when the first deal
> may have cost Liora
> everything.)

The jaguar s t r e t c h e s lazily
on the burnt ground.
*I won't tell the first girl you love or the second*
> *(if you find her)*
*about your past.*
*I won't tell them about your bargain*
*with Death.*
*But look at the souls here;*
*look how* exposed *they are.*

*Do you really think*
*you can avoid the same fate?*

Well.
I can *try*.

**The brittle trees begin to snap and wail**
in winds that died off a hundred years ago,
and I bend
my head against their cries.

Lights wink through the gale,
fallen gems from some long-gone king's crown.
They waltz with each other,
their song sweet.
*Andres*, they call, *Andres*.

With each whisper of my name,
my feet shift
farther off the path, closer to the lights.
Their glow feels familiar—
a soft kiss, a soothing hand.
They sound like everything
torn away from me;
calm nights unbroken by cries and curses,
a home where all of me is welcome,
peace, and Liora, Liora, Liora.

And as her name
floats into my mind,
I catch the sparkle of ballet shoes
turned up *en pointe*.

The slippers belong to a girl
standing beneath a dogwood tree.
Her golden hair lances through the air,
a ray of sunlight
I've threaded my fingers in before.

*Liora*, I breathe.

Liora takes first position, second, third,
all edges and elegance.
*Andres*, she sighs. *You're here!*
*You came!*
*Please, help me!*
Liora holds her arms out, desperate
for a partner.

*No, Andres!* snarls the jaguar.
              (Forever
                    untrusting and untrustworthy.)

But I streak past her, fast as the shadow
I abandoned.
              (Or tried to.)

I'll carry Liora home if I have to,
like a mermaid whose feet will bleed
with every mortal step she takes.

I'll complete our circle again, weave the cords
of our lives into a single chain
that won't snap
because of a parent, an accident, a tragedy.

                                If I can reach Liora,
I can undo my mistake and repair
the hairline fractures in all three of us.
I can—

**Renee's arms encircle my waist.**
*Andres, stop!* she shouts
over the symphony of love found.
*That isn't Liora!*
*It's an illusion, a whirlpool*
*trying to pull you in!*
*You can't go*
*to whatever that is!*

Liora's eyes
brim with luminous tears.
*Don't listen to her!* she begs.
*I'm no one but myself!*

*Liar!* Renee counters.
*And I can prove it.*
The flash
her camera creates is tiny;
the gloom engulfs it
almost as soon as it spreads.

But the photo
the Polaroid spits at our feet
is like Liora's name: all light.
In it, our girlfriend has swallowed
a whole galaxy.
She is beautiful, a girl-shaped miracle.
And she

       is

           *wrong.*

I curl my fingers inward
before I can touch
the thing that's twisted itself into Liora.

Our girlfriend is *human*; she isn't a nebula
compressed into something smaller,
less important.
She's enough on her own.
And the cut of this creature's smile
is so jagged it could wreck ships.
How did I ever mistake a siren
for a mermaid?

Standing tall, standing *firm*, I say,
*You're not Liora.*

The girl made of light and her smile
break.
Not like morning
rushing over city streets,
but like a mirror
smashed in anger.
And the thing
        (false and fae)
that isn't Liora flickers out
as I collapse into Renee.
        (And safety.)

**The two of us lie on the parched ground,**
panting.
Averting a disaster is exhausting;
nearly being the cause of one
drains you down to the marrow.

Guilt makes my apology stick in my lungs
for longer than I'd like.
At last, I say to Renee,
*I'm sorry I didn't listen to you;*
*I was being foolish.*
*Thank you for saving me.*

Renee stares at me
like I've used a language
she's struggling to translate.
Then she breathes out
s l o w l y,
disturbing the flakes of ash on her lashes—
souvenirs
from the ever-dying forest.
*You're welcome.*

*Those were the Yara lights*
*your uncle told you about, weren't they?* I ask.
*The ones that try to lure travelers*
*off the path?*

*I think so, yes.*
Renee picks at her nail polish;
strips of it
fall to the ground, joining the river's ghost.
*Andres, I understand*
*why you wanted to believe the Yara lights*
*were Liora.*
*A part of me did too.*
*But not everything that glitters here*
*means us well.*

I nod.
If the Yara lights are in these woods,
how many other monsters
call this place *home*?

*I'll be more careful,* I promise.
*You won't have to rescue me*
*twice.*


**We pull ourselves off the ground**
and continue into the forest.
But no amount of distance
can erase the false Liora's razor blade smile
or the tears she wore
like stolen jewelry.


The crooked vision of the girl we love
stays lodged in my skin and brain—
and Renee must sense it.
        She asks,
*Are you okay, Andres?*


I want to lie; I want to reassure her
I'm *fine.*
But the tears I've tried so hard to trap
work themselves free.
This time, I don't bother wiping them away.
So what
if I'm salt and sorrow?
Everything else here is.

*You saw the same thing I did—*
*Liora broken*
*in that bed!* I cry.
*She was more fracture*
*than girl!*
*Every time*
*I remember, I want to scream.*
*But you, you're so* calm.
*How?*

*I* have *to stay calm!* Renee fires back.
*If I don't,*
*I'll become a cry on the wind,*
*one of the trees rooted to this place*
*by grief.*
*So forgive me*
*for putting Liora first—*
*and not my own feelings.*

Renee stomps past me
on her black velvet heels.
Her peacock's colors gutter in and out,
dazzling to dim,
as he follows.
He shows his pain
the way my girlfriend won't.

I caused this—with my temper.
I caused this—with the deal I struck,
robbing the living world of Liora.

Slowly, I unwrap
my fists.
Dante was right.
This *is* the land where nothing shines;
even the stars
reject it.
And the ones on my palms
are so dark
they devour all other light.

I was supposed to be better
than this.

# CHAPTER
## TWENTY-ONE

**The dead trees give way**
and the Yara lights are replaced by the dull glimmer
of the City.

Some other boy
from some other part of the world
where children grow up dazzled by snowfall
might see the City's gates
as the yawning mouth of a wolf, a cougar, an orca.

But I can't shake Miami.
I see an alligator, its teeth and scales blackened
by an eternity of rot.
The animal's spine and tail
form the walls of the City;
its vertebrae scrape the blank sky.

I gawk at the skeleton, death encasing death.
*Please tell me*
*you're seeing*
*what* I'm *seeing*, I whisper to Renee.

My girlfriend rolls a yellow notch of bone
between her fingers.
*Which great hero took down this monster—*
*whatever it really looked like*
*when it was still alive*
*and not shaped by a hundred imaginations?* she wonders.
*Was it Theseus? Hercules?*
*The twins, Hunahpu and Xbalanque?*

Then Renee's hand drops to her side.
The shadow-girl I glimpsed
(both morbid and curious)
steps back behind the curtain.
And I'm left with my flame-girl again.

**The peacock and jaguar don't approach the gates.**
They remain
at the edge of the woods, ready to plunge
back into the trees.

*Aren't you coming with us?* I say.

The peacock shakes his head.
*This is the oldest city in creation.*
*The first one, built with souls*
*instead of shovels.*

*But unlike cities in the living world,*
*it is entirely human.*
*And we do not belong there.*

The jaguar adds,
*You might want to reconsider*
*going through those gates yourselves,*
            *little*

                  *living*

                        *things.*
*There's no guarantee*
*you'll come back out again.*
*The City has a way*
*of ensnaring human beings.*

Renee dismisses this advice
with a flick of her wrist.
*We have to go on.*
*But thank you*
*for all your help.*

I wrench my own thanks out.
(Grudgingly.)
*Yes.*
*We're grateful to you.*

But the peacock isn't done
with us.
*If you should ever find yourself*
*lost in a moment*
*when you can't see the path ahead,*

*you may call on us*
*to help you—*
*even if you are within*
*the walls of the City.*

*But you only call on us*
*once,* says the jaguar.

*Why only once?* I protest.

*How many wishes can you make*
*on a single star?* the peacock asks in return.
*How many times can you strike*
*the same match?*
*Even magic has its limits.*
His gaze
perches on Renee.
*You already know* that.

Renee purses her lips around a story
whose pages she shares with her peacock . . .
and her peacock alone.

I bite back
a dozen questions;
they burn as they settle in my belly.
Now I understand Renee's frustration
with my secrets—
and the ones Liora may have tucked away
on the other side of her smile.

*Good*, says the peacock.
       *Luck*, concludes the jaguar.

I blink, and the animals
(the light and the silhouette it casts)
are gone.

**I stride forward to open the gates—**
but Renee presses a hand to my chest,
giving me a warning
of her own.
*Switch off the melody of your heart;*
*dim the light in your eyes.*
*We need to blend in.*
*If the dead know we're alive,*
*they might try to follow us home—*
*or worse.*

Can I hide what's most human about me
when *human* is all I've ever been?
I have to try—
for me and Renee, for Liora.

The two of us
       (Dante in heels,
       Odysseus without his tricks,
       a triangle with only one side intact)
walk through the City gates.

# CHAPTER
## TWENTY-TWO

**Rain bombards the City of the dead—**
an endless invader
waging a successful siege.

       It crawls
down the sides of the buildings—
the bones of New York, Chicago, Hong Kong
somehow carried here.
Each window is fogged over, hiding the unending
afterlives of the dead.

The souls in the City
wear clothes from every era.
There are bell-bottoms
       (their hems soaked),
dapper pinstripe suits
       (studded with raindrops
       in place of diamonds),

and flowing Victorian gowns.
       (Their high lace collars
       prick at the skin like frost.)

The dead don't turn our way
or notice
how the damp air trips in our lungs;
they don't call us *stranger*, *interloper*.
Like the living,
they're too preoccupied with their own business
to pay attention to ours.

All the colors here
are dark and rough:
the blue of a sky bruised by a hurricane,
the gray of bullets fired decades ago.
The streetlights burn
in harsh whites,
and the eyes of the people who pass by
are extensions of the rain.
Their irises
come in deep purple verging on black,
ash gray, smoke silver.

*Liora must hate it here*, Renee says
as we dip under a battered awning.
*She loves the light,*
*whether it comes from the sun or the moon.*
*She loves warm colors*
*and glowing afternoons.*

*And the City*
*doesn't have* any *of those things.*

I put my arm around Renee.
If I can't erase the shadows
slinking up my arms,
I can try to shield her from the others here.

*When Liora wakes up, we'll help her forget*
*about this place*, I declare.
*We'll bring balloons, a rainbow of macarons.*
*We'll paint prisms*
*on her walls.*

The wind
tries to steal Renee's laughter.
*You can't draw, Andres!*
*And neither can I.*

*It's the thought that counts*, I argue.
*Liora will enjoy*
*our stick figures, our cartoon animals,*
*our fake van Gogh stars.*
I lower my head, kissing Renee
hard enough to make us *both* forget
where we are.

It's much better
than a sip of the River Lethe.

**We dodge the trams**
creeping past us like wounded animals;
we dart around graying souls.
Block after block, only one thing remains constant:
the posters
clinging to every building, window, fence.

I thought the underworld,
with its circles, layers, and rooftops,
would be governed by Death herself.
But apparently, the City has another ruler.
One I didn't meet
six months ago.

The posters show this ruler
bestowing kisses like favors.
The touch of his lips
turns tears to wide-eyed bliss.
Most of his face is lost
in darkness; its his grin, sharpened by ambition,
that shines.

And on every poster
is one phrase, one title, one introduction:
*the Prince,*
  *the Prince,*
    *the Prince*
      *in the dark.*

*Did your grandmother*
*mention anything about this Prince?* I ask Renee.
*Did your uncle*
*ever talk about him?*

Her grimace
is answer enough.
*Princes were notably absent*
*from all my uncle's stories.*
*As for my grandmother . . .*
*she warned me*
*never to come here at all.*

# CHAPTER
## TWENTY-THREE

**A boy with a gold earring and umber skin**
stands on the nearest street corner,
undeterred by the downpour.

Renee and I haven't spoken to anyone here;
we haven't dared to.
But the stack of newspapers
in the boy's arms feels promising.

*If there's a prince here,*
*there might be a government*, I suggest.
*And governments*
*love making lists of comings and goings.*
*Liora could be on one.*

Rain collects at the corners of Renee's frown.
*That seems too easy,*
*too organized,*

*for the chaos of this place.*
*But maybe, we could learn something*
*from a newspaper.*

We've barely begun to move toward the boy
when he thrusts a paper at Renee.
*Stories, stories!* he announces.
*All the most important stories!*

One headlines states,
> *RUMOR HAS IT*
> *THE BEST IS YET TO COME.*

Another declares,
> *RUMOR HAS IT*
> *THE WORST IS YET TO COME.*

And on the paper's last page,
the Prince has left his mark again
in bold ink.
> *THE PRINCE WILL GIVE*
> *HIS FORGETFUL KISS*
> *TO SEVEN LUCKY PEOPLE*
> *AT THE STROKE OF TWELVE TONIGHT.*
> *WHO*
> > *WILL*
> > > *THOSE LUCKY PEOPLE*
> > > > *BE?*

Renee glares at the newsprint.
The words leave black scars on her fingers,
like she too is carrying her share
            of shadows.
*Who is this Prince?* Renee asks the boy.
*And why would anyone*
*want his kiss?*

The boy
            (eighteen or eighty?
            It's impossible to tell)
flicks the corner of the newspaper.
*You must be new arrivals!*
*Or haven't you heard?*
*The River Lethe*
            (*our one chance at peace!*)
*is gone.*
*Or maybe it was reborn*
*in the Prince.*
*A kiss from him will make you forget*
*everything that happened*
*up there.*
He points, clandestine,
to the dismal sky and the world
we all left.
            (Or were forced out of.)
*And isn't that for the best?*

Renee's edges crackle.
In the City, where thoughts are king,
could she combust like a true phoenix
if she were angry enough?
        (Can *I*
            if the infection of shadows
            reaches my brain, my heart,
            some other vital organ?)

*You're wrong*, Renee tells the boy.
*Forgetting doesn't heal anyone;*
*it won't bring you peace.*
*Only moving out of this City*
        *(only moving* on)
*can do that.*

The boy
snatches his newspaper from her.
*You don't know anything!* he snaps.

I place my hand
on Renee's waist to steady her—
body, soul, and otherwise.
(Thanks to Mami,
I've had plenty of practice.)
*Ignore him*, I whisper.
*Can you really blame the dead*
*for believing they need that kiss?*
*We've all wanted to forget our mistakes*
*at one point or another.*

*You're right.*
Renee closes her eyes,
raindrops twining in ribbons
down her cheeks.
Everyone here is always weeping—
whether they know it or not.
*We all have parts of our lives*
*we wish we could wash away.*

# CHAPTER
## TWENTY-FOUR

**We enter the next building we come to:**
a coal-stained hotel,
its swiftly revolving doors and unsmiling bellhop
smudged with gray.

But it's not the rain driving us inside;
it's another theory of Renee's.
*Hotels are way stations, not homes,* she says.
*They're spaces between*
*one place and another,*
*just like Liora's between places*
*herself.*
*Maybe she came here to wait.*

*For what?* I ask.

Renee lifts her shoulders.
*For whatever comes next.*

**The hotel's lobby is too crowded—with spirits, voices . . .**
and posters advertising a singer.
She's an impression of a girl
in barely dried oil paints.
Her features are veiled
by swirling rainbows of light,
making her the inverse of the Prince
in every way.

*Come and hear*
*the City's newest wonder!*
the posters declare in golden letters.

Renee and I turn from the forest of posters
toward the front desk,
where the dead press up against one another
like books on a shelf.
We tangle ourselves
in this crowd, curiosity our joint vice.

Above the heads of the City residents,
I can just make out
the bronze plaque on the desk.
It's gone green from rain and the ages,
but I can still read what it says:
*The Dead Letter Office.*

The cries of the many souls
form a single plea.

*Please let me send*
*this letter, this note, this one last message*
*to the world above!*
*Please see that it reaches the living!*

The postman behind the desk
accepts each letter with a nod . . . or a yawn.
I think he's heard it all before;
I think he'll hear it all again.

(What's compassion fatigue?
Seeing so much pain
you go winter numb
to all of it.)

**My girlfriend and I ride the swell of the spirits**
up to the postman.
Renee leans halfway across the desk,
mindful of the letters stacked on it.
*You haven't received a note*
*from a new arrival*
*named Liora, have you?* she asks.

The postman's weary voice
drags itself from his throat.
*Miss*, he says,
*I don't read the letters; I only collect them.*

My brows and heartbeat
rise in unison.
*Collect them?*
*You don't* send *them?*

*Where would I send them?* asks the postman.
*We exist*
*in the land of nowhere.*
*We can't reach the living—*
*and the living can't reach* us.
*The letters are for you—*
*to say one last word, give one last goodbye,*
*get closure as best you can.*

*No! That can't be!*
A boy our age lunges at the desk,
tears dripping down his face
as his damp hair
drips into his eyes.
*Please*, he begs the postman.
*I need my sister to know*
*I love her!*
*I need to let her know it wasn't her fault*
*I couldn't stay.*
He holds his letter tightly,
the way he must have held his sister's hand
in life.

Could Renee and I take the note
back with us when
        (if)
we leave?
*Maybe. . . .*

Renee's thoughts and my own are in harmony;
she doesn't need to me finish.
*Nothing here is real,*
*remember?* she reminds me.
*It's built from dreams and nightmares—*
*and that includes*
*the boy's letter.*
*We can't help him, Andres.*
*He can only help* himself.

My girlfriend loops her arm in mine,
a key that's found its lock.
        (The only thing we have
        after losing the world we knew
        is each other.)

As we leave
the postman, the boy, his unsent letter,
I say,
*When I saw the City gates,*
*I thought*
*it would be frightening here.*
*I didn't ever think*
*it would be this sad.*

*It* is *sad*, Renee says softly.
*As long as these people stay here,*
*none of them will ever get the second chance*
*they want.*

She's right.
The faded people in the lobby
are a hundred Eleanor Rigbys, lonely and half forgotten.

*This might be selfish . . .*
*but I'm glad*
*you and I*
*don't belong here*, I murmur to Renee.

(But what if, thanks to me, Liora *does*?)

**We ask everyone we can about our girlfriend.**
And each time we do,
the dead give variations of the same answer
in slightly different keys.

> *(I haven't seen anyone like that.*

> > *I don't know*
> > *who you're talking about.*

> > > *Go away and leave me*
> > > *alone!)*

Renee and I share another sigh,
watching the latest soul
flit away across the lobby.
But as my gaze snags on a new spirit,
my breath stills—
the way Renee instructed it to
at the gates.

A man is pinning up a new poster
of the radiant singing girl.
He's spilling out of himself
in June yellows and the softest greens of May;
his fingertips and eyes weep the same colors
as the paintbrush
tucked behind his bandaged ear.

I never met this man
in life;
I know him just the same,
even without
the heart-shaped wound in his chest,
a scar to match the others he carried
all his days on earth.

I lead Renee
closer to the painter, in free fall through history.
*Excuse me*, I stammer,
*but are you*
*the artist of these posters?*

Vincent van Gogh
      (long gone, 1853–1890)
flattens the palm of his left hand
on the back of his right,
trying to stave off
a flood of star-blue paint.
He can't be the real van Gogh, bleeding color
right before our eyes . . .
      yet
            he
                  is.

*I'm the painter, yes*, says Vincent.
*But I haven't captured my subject*
*quite right yet.*
*My work is still imperfect—and I can't*
      *let*
            *it*
                  *be.*

*The girl in this painting*
*makes things grow!*
*Her irises and sunflowers,*
*poppies and plum blossoms*
*are the first flowers I've ever seen bloom*
*in the City.*
*She feels like* life *did.*
*So my paintings of her*
*needs to as well.*

*Like life?* Renee and I gasp.
We're a fusion of hope and fear,
faith and disbelief.

Could the shining girl Vincent van Gogh painted
be Liora?
Or are we trying to find meaning
in a place that has none?

*Wait!* Renee starts.
*Please tell us—*

It's too late.
Vincent van Gogh is already gone, borne away
by the rain and the crowd.
All that's left of him
is a drop of paint
on the marble floor.

Beside us, a new laugh
dances through the air.
*Never expect a straight answer*
*from an artist!* the smiling voice says.
*You're bound to be disappointed*
*if you do.*

Renee and I spin and finally see someone
who *looks* marked
by their death.

# CHAPTER
## TWENTY-FIVE

**The boy who spoke to us is covered in scars.**
His blue football jersey
has melted to his lean body;
most of his skin is charred black,
curling
at the corners to reveal
the bony ridges of his chin, his shoulders,
the basket of his ribs.
His hair is untamed fire, a sunset
riding over the horizon.

This boy wants everyone to know
how he came to the City.

(Is that admirable or not?)

*You're alive*, the boy says,
stating what should be obvious
to the other City dwellers.
   (And isn't.)
His accent
belongs to a country of sunflowers
I've never set foot in.
*How are you here*
*if you're alive?*

**Renee meets the dead boy**
head-on.
If she could transform herself
into one of her tarot cards,
she'd be Strength,
prying open
the lion's mouth to fill it with honey.
*We've come looking*
*for our girlfriend.*

Our *girlfriend?*
The boy with the scars snorts.
*What are you, communists?*
*Running a collective*
*of love?*

I fold my arms across my chest.
   (As a means of protection
   or intimidation?
   I can't say.)

*That's much more creative*
*than the insults*
*other teens have shouted.*

*I've known bricks with more creativity*
*than other teenagers.*
The boy's tone is Mojave dry.
But he's no xerophyte, no cactus kid,
his arms spread like angel wings.
No one in the City can be.
A xerophyte
would drown in this climate.

Renee eyes the boy, trying to read his age
like the rings of a tree
cut down too soon.
*You don't look much older*
*than us.*

The boy laughs.
*I'm not.*
*I graduated from life in March 2022,*
*in the city of Mariupol,*
*thanks to Vladimir Putin, the Russian army,*
*and their missiles.*
He points to his face,
a map of old suffering.
*I keep these*
*because I want to remember*
*what was done to me,*
*my country, my friends, my family.*

*But not everyone here*
*chooses* to *remember.*
*Some of us are desperate*
*to forget.*

So desperate they drank
the River Lethe
dry.
So desperate they scramble
for the kiss of the Prince
in the dark.

*I'm sorry*, Renee and I say.
We're *sorry for your loss.*

The boy's ravaged mouth
twists
in a smile too soft for the rest of him.
*So*

        *am*

            *I.*

**The boy may wear his history proudly,**
but he's quick to circle back to us
and the present.
He asks,
*What's your girlfriend like?*

How to describe Liora?
I'm a musician in love; I should know how.

But tonight, my words
slip out of reach.

A stray raindrop
falls on Ariel's strings,
sustaining a long A, high and candied.
I follow her lead.

*Our girlfriend sings hope
into something you can almost hold*, I say.
*She could dance spring back to life
after a long winter.*

I expect the scarred boy to laugh
at this fairy-dust image of a girl.
But his bones clink and clang
as he shifts
from one burnt sneaker
to
       the
              other.
Is he getting ready to run—from us
and this conversation?

The boy taps van Gogh's poster,
his crooked fingers
winding over the shimmering letters.
*Vincent isn't exaggerating
what this girl can do, the kind of power
she has.*

*When she sings and dances,*
*things do come back to life.*
*But if that's the girl*
*you came here looking for,*
*you should turn back now.*

Renee narrows her eyes, her look so dark
it matches her shoes.
*Why?*

The dead boy shrugs.
His shoulders move like the sea,
lapping at this world
and the one he was forced to shed.
*Because she belongs to someone*
*you don't want to steal from.*
*My suggestion, kids?*
*Go back above, to the places*
*where flowers grow on their own.*
*You'll join this Liora*
                *(wherever she is)*
*soon enough.*
*Or hasn't anyone ever told you*
*how short life really is?*

*We're not leaving,* we say.
*Please tell us—*
*who has the singing girl?*

*The Prince*, the boy chants.
*The Prince in the dark.*
> (But is it a prayer to summon this ruler . . .
> or to keep him away?)
*The one with oblivion*
*in his kiss.*


**The boy slings an arm around me,**
as if we've already shared
a cradle, a football field, jokes
only the two of us can understand.
As if we're already friends.
*I know you want to hear more*
*about the Prince.*
*But the City's depressing enough*
*without bringing monsters*
*into the mix.*
He looks from me to Renee,
his hair tickling my cheeks.
(It too smells like fire.)
*Are the two of you sure*
*you won't change your minds*
*and go home?*


*We won't,* I say.
> *We never will,* adds Renee.

The boy's chuckle
crackles from between his broken teeth.
*The living are usually cowards*
*who don't understand*
*how good they have it.*
*But you two seem different.*
*You came here*
*to beat odds that can't be beaten,*
*light up a darkness*
*no one can cut through.*
*If you want,*
*I'll take you to the singing girl.*
*But I won't go any farther*
*than that.*
He holds up a warped hand.
*I won't risk what's left of me*
*for strangers.*
*So,*

> *what*

> > *do you*

> > > *say?*

*Only if*, I say.

> *You give us your name*, Renee finishes.

The boy twirls past me—
and our demand.
*Call me Virgil*, he offers.
*It's as good a name as any.*
*And it's fitting for a guide,*
*isn't it?*

Another lesson from the underworld:
if you bargain with the Other,
cut a deal with a faerie,
be prepared
for them to find loopholes.

# CHAPTER
## TWENTY-SIX

**Virgil, the beacon in the gray,**
takes us through the streets,
his skeletal hands shoved in his pockets—
a casual attempt
at being the boy he was
and not the specter
he is.

The farther we travel,
the uncannier the City becomes,
and I begin to recognize
too many of the people here.

Amy Winehouse has chosen a home in the City
after her life
changed hands with her death.

She plays
on a street corner to a crowd of onlookers,
despair pumping in her lungs
instead of air.
Beside her, Elvis Presley shimmies and shakes;
he's young again, forever and always.

I can't help staring . . .
and Virgil can't help laughing.
*Jimi Hendrix is a resident too,* he tells me.
*And so is Marilyn Monroe.*
*David Bowie gave his last few concerts here*
*before sailing away*
*on a wave of glitter and guitar riffs.*
He plucks Ariel's strings, teasing
a few notes from her.
*Bowie took Kurt Cobain with him.*
*For a lark, I guess.*
*It just goes to show*
*Death doesn't care if you're famous . . .*
*or not.*
*She's fair—and we're all finite.*

I can see his point.
But how fair can Death be
when she snuffed out a light like Liora
for *me*?

**There's more than longing in the City—**
there's something sharper too.
I see it lurking
at the mouths of alleyways,
on the thresholds of buildings,
in doorways crooked like fingers,
inviting me inside.

But I see it most of all
in a cluster of men
beneath the white eye of a streetlamp.
They have a different texture
than the other souls here.
It's not the woolen heaviness of sorrow
smothering them;
these men feel like cold silk.

They wear a uniform of a kind:
tan jackets, bowler hats, twentieth-century echoes.
They're a wake of vultures
hunched over ruins.
They're a committee of pain,
their smiles sickle-edged.
Someone else's screams
are coiled at the backs of their throats;
someone else's tears
are gathered at the corners of their eyes.

I don't want to stray.
But the points of the black stars on my palms
stretch to meet my wrists . . .
and the vulture men ahead.

I break from Renee
and go to them.

**Living boy, living boy,** the vulture men say.
*We wondered*
*when you'd arrive.*
*Though we expected you to be dead*
*when you did.*

*How do you know me?* I ask.

*We don't,* reply the vulture men.
*But we've heard of you.*

*Because I'm alive?*
            (Can a rumor really move as fast
            as the rain does here?)

The vulture men skulk toward me,
trying to cinch their circle
closed.
But I step back from these predators.
This game is old—and I used to be an expert
at it.

I won't be trapped, cornered;
I won't be forced to fight
my way out.

      (Even if a part of me
      *wants* to throw a punch, a snarl,
      a slashing remark at these men.
      Even if a part of me
      wants to unleash the heat
      swelling in my hands.)

The vulture men purr,
*We all recognize you, Andres Santos.*
*And soon, others will too.*
*Shadows call*
*to other shadows.*

*I don't know*
*what you're talking about.*
My lie is clean,
a cut made by a scalpel.
But it doesn't fool the vulture men.

*You do*, they insist. *You're like us . . .*
*even if you won't admit it.*

One of the vultures taps my wrist,
trying to ease my fist open.
      (Trying to reveal the secret
      he must already know.)

*I don't*, I begin—
and end just as quickly.

> Every end is a beginning in the making.
> (Especially in this place.)

**Virgil grabs me by the collar,**
the older brother
I never had, and tears me away
from the cluster of slinking, smirking men.

*See you soon*, the vulture men call
as Virgil and I make our hasty retreat.

Our guide delivers me back to Renee,
but his attention
is still held by the men
swarming under the lamppost.

Virgil points back at them,
the way a knight would point his sword
at a dragon.
*Contrary to popular belief*
> *(on earth, anyway),*
*most souls in the City*
*aren't bad, he explains.*
*They aren't even weak.*
*You saw the people trying to mail letters,*
*didn't you?*

*We did,* says Renee.
*We felt sorry for them.*

*You should,* Virgil replies.
*The guilt and regret they feel*
            *(for being dead,*
                *for being imperfect, for being* human)
*keeps them pinned to the pavement here.*
*But there are some people*
*who deserve to carry their disgrace*
*like a pocketful of stones.*

*They're monsters.*
*Monsters who leveled cities,*
*blew up lives,*
*starved their neighbors of happiness.*
*Monsters who believed*
*they were sweeping the world clean*
*of mistakes.*
*But mistakes are all*
*they*
*ever*
*made.*
*There's famous—*
*and then there's in*famous.

*But who were they, exactly?* Renee presses.
*In life?*

Virgil swipes away a drop of rain.

(And holds back
a shudder.)

*The ones*
*who lined girls up*
*against the walls of soccer stadiums*
*for protesting, wearing nail polish, fighting back.*
*The ones*
*who dragged men, women, children*
*into pine forests and shot them*
*for the crime*
*of their bloodline and their faith.*
*The ones*
*who dropped bombs and broke the world*
*instead of building it up.*
*Don't fuck with the vultures, kids.*
*They've eaten too many of the living*
*already.*


And they believe I'm one of them.
If I rolled up my sleeve, how much of me
would still *be* me—
and not the worst of who I am?


I tighten my grip on Ariel's neck,
breathing deep.
I don't want to belong
with the vulture men.
But if I sold a girl's life
for my own peace of mind,
maybe I earned my guilt, the black stars, the pain
found in both.

# CHAPTER
## TWENTY-SEVEN

**The mist crowds us the way the departed don't.**
It unspools outward, a trail for us to follow.

But the fog's icy fingers
can't banish
the sweat beading along my forehead.
The encounter with the vulture men
did me no favors; my hands are warmer
than ever.

And they grow hotter still
as Renee says,
*Virgil told us*
*this is the kingdom of regrets, of guilt.*
*But what did Liora feel guilty about?*
*What wasn't she telling us*
*about her life*

*that could have stalked her*
*to the edge of death?*

My feet skid on the damp pavement.
*What do you mean?*

*Mrs. Rose shouldn't have known*
*you and I existed . . .*
*but she clearly hated us*, says Renee.
*Liora never stayed out late,*
*but she was hit by a car*
*close to midnight.*

*She could have gone*
*for a walk—*
*and Miami drivers are reckless*, I offer.
*They treat their cars*
*like rocket ships.*
*They think they can outrace*
*the phases of the moon, spirits, their own thoughts.*

Renee threads her fingers
through her hair, tangling it further.
*That's not the point, Andres!*
*The pieces of herself Liora showed us*
*and the rest of her life*

        *don't*

            *add*

                *up*

*to a soul*

*like Vincent van Gogh's, Virgil's,*
*that boy's, with his unsent letter.*
*To any soul trapped here.*

Virgil swings back to us.
He may be a patchwork boy,
but he moves with easy grace.
*Maybe the two of you*
*didn't know this girlfriend of yours*
*as well as you thought*, he says.
*Maybe her secrets*
*hunted and haunted her*
*to her grave.*

*Just because* you're *dead*
*doesn't mean Liora is!*
I try to the take back the words
as soon as they crawl
out of my mouth.
But I can't inhale or unmake them;
in life or in death,
breath doesn't work that way.

    (What's wrong with me?
    What is this place *doing* to me?)

If Virgil is upset, he lets the feeling tumble
off his back, along with the rain.
*I was doing just fine*
*until the Russians came*, he replies.

# CHAPTER
## TWENTY-EIGHT

**The theater Virgil takes us to**
is a living-dead threnody.

Ash is scattered on the marble steps
leading to the gold-gilded doors.
Rubble lies on the sidewalk;
the Roman columns holding up the remnants
of the roof
wear bullet wounds, ascending and descending
like a scale.

Boys must have sat on these steps
and written odes
to the ones they loved.
Ballerinas must have built
stories with their bodies on its stage.

Brujas must have cast dice in the attic
to read the future
and come up with destruction as the outcome
every time.

The building is grander
than anything we've seen in the City.
(So far.)
But it shares one thing in common
with the squat blocks of apartment buildings
and crooked towers:
it feels heavy, like it's grieving
the people it had to abandon
when it was destroyed
in the world above.

Renee tips her head back,
taking in
the theater's impressive scope.
(And decay.)
*This place is amazing!*

*Some things in the City are,* Virgil concedes.
*It's not just people and trees that die;*
*buildings do too.*
*The important ones, anyway.*
*And this one is* still *important.*
*It's where the girl*
*who brings things to life*
*sings.*

Is that girl Liora?
I hope she is; I hope she isn't.
I wanted more people to see her magic . . .
but not when she's trapped
in the prison of a prince's selfish hands.

I hurtle past my fears and say,
*What happened to the theater?*
*How did it die?*
(I've been all questions and no answers
since meeting Virgil.)

Virgil pauses
on the theater's second step.
His left ankle is skinned
past the pink muscle, all the way
to the bone.
*It died in a war, I think.*
*Not mine, but someone else's.*
*One that ended*
*before the three of us were even hints*
*in our parents' eyes.*

There's always a war to fight.
(Somewhere.)
Inside or outside
a house, a body, a spirit.

**Sorrow's infectious here,**
and Renee and I are huddled too close
not to catch each other's melancholy
like a cold.

Rubbing at her elbows, Renee says,
*I want Liora to be inside.*
*But I'm also afraid she is.*
*What if this Prince*
*is holding her hostage, a black hole*
*feeding on a star?*

I sprinkle kisses on Renee's cheeks,
hoping to make them warmer
than the rain would allow otherwise.
*If the Prince has Liora,*
*we'll rescue her.*
*We've got to have more power*
*than the dead.*
            (Don't we?)
*So, are you ready?*

Renee won't commit.
But she starts up the stairs
and into
whatever comes next.

**Inside the theater, everything reeks of burnt timber**
and the wicked hint of gunpowder.
The floorboards and velvet curtains
are scarred black with bomb residue.

The impossible scent of cigarette smoke
wafts through the air, a dream
set on fire.

In this crumbling place,
the City has created music of its own:
glasses clink, heels tap,
a cry catches in someone's throat.
But this won't ever be a melody
I can dance to, love to, fall into.

At the base of the stage, sepia-toned lovers
try to kiss the red
back into one another's mouths.
Some almost succeed,
their lips turning candy pink.
Groups of friends attempt to laugh
dead roses back into bloom.
But their petals stay a stubborn gray.

None of the people in the theater
speak above a whisper,
as if this place is too holy to house
more than that.
But I still hear
snatches of conversation,
prayers for better days, wishes made on a shadow.
(Not a star.)

*I heard the Prince*
*will give*
*another seven kisses tonight.*

> *I hope he chooses me.*
> *If I could forget my life,*
> *I could be happy in death.*

> > *If only we still had Lethe*
> > *and not just some boy's kiss!*

Virgil takes us past these rumors
and up to the bar.
It's crowded with glasses of rainwater
pretending to be
pink lemonade and Guinness.

I collapse
on a splintered leather stool,
kneading at the bridge of my nose as I battle
a headache that shouldn't be.

If forgetfulness, a single song from a girl
          (maybe from Liora, maybe not),
and a kiss
are all the dead have to look forward to,
I think
Renee's grandmother was wrong
about the City.

I think
this must be Hell after all.

# CHAPTER
## TWENTY-NINE

**Virgil notices me and Renee**
measuring
the people in the theater with our eyes, weighing them
against *him*.

For the second time,
he slings his bone-threaded arm around me
so we stand hip to hip.
The feel of him
should make my skin want to creep away.
It doesn't.

> (How Virgil died isn't his fault.
> He didn't set out to spend his eternity
> as a scarred jester.)

*I know, I know.* Virgil laughs.
*I'm different*
*from most of the others.*

*Why though?*
Renee tugs
on a coil of Virgil's fiery hair.
The lens of her camera flares
as it tries to snatch the truth from him.
*Why aren't you clamoring*
*for the Prince's kiss too?*

*Because I don't regret*
*any part of my life.*
*So why*
*should I want to forget it?*
Virgil grins, kicking his worn sneakers
onto on the bar,
two shocking slices of red.

The bartender glares
at the dead boy,
Virgil's scars, his full spectrum of scarlet hues.
*What are* you *doing here?* the bartender demands.
He SLAMS
the glass he was cleaning on the counter,
trembling flakes of ash
freeing themselves from his fine hair.
*You don't belong!*
*You'll scare away*
*the other customers.*

*I'm entitled to be here,*
*to try to remember*
*what sour cherry juice or vodka tastes like,*

*to hear the Prince's girl sing*
*just as much as anyone else*, Virgil replies.
*You can't throw me out—*
*I haven't caused any trouble.*
But I hear the taunt
our guide won't come out and say:
*Yet.*

The woman beside him
swivels on her seat,
the hem of her moth-eaten dress
flapping against my knees.
Her eyes are tombstones, cold and gray.
*You don't need to hear* her *sing.*
*And you don't want the Prince's kiss*, she argues.
*If you did,*
*you wouldn't be walking around like* that,
*full of holes and memories.*
She stabs her finger—at Virgil,
then Renee and me.
*You don't belong here!*
*And neither do the living tourists!*

The word *living*
sends a ripple through the theater—
and too many heads
turn our way.
The jealousy of the City's citizens
makes moss-green undertones surface
on their skin, a brief respite
from their monotone existence.

Of course, they envy our possibilities.
They're film-strip souls:
they can't go any further
than their last reel.

I surprise myself
by giving the crowd my middle finger,
the tip coated in shadow.
I wish
I were a castle, a hillside, a river.
Then I could hide
Renee from their eyes—and their envy.

But Renee only sighs
at our audience.
*Ignore them.*
*They're just—*

*Jealous,* I mutter.
*I know.*

**A stranger at the bar knocks over his glass.**
It streams onto the floor,
a runaway tale.
But the man ignores it, his attention consumed
by Renee.

*I know you!* the stranger cries.
He stumbles to her, pawing at her hands,
seeking the comfort of a heart
that isn't rusted shut.

*You look just like my wife!*
*You must be her!*
*I've waited*
*so long to be reunited!*
*Even without the Prince's kiss,*
*we can have peace now—if only*
*we stay together.*

But none of that is true.
This man doesn't match
Renee's soul.
His hair is platinum, not ruby red;
his ribs rise from his shirt
like towers.
He is thin and white, nobility
eaten away by time or fame.

Renee tries to shift
closer to me, away from the desperate man.
As a boy,
I've never felt the electric wave of panic
sparked
from being pinned by hungry eyes.
But I still recognize it.

*I'm not your wife*, says Renee.
*Please, leave me alone.*

But the man doesn't.
He caresses her cheek, a net
about to ensnare a mermaid.

And I—

**—grab the man's wrist before he can.**
*She told you to stop!* I snarl, all subtropical heat,
January
in the southern hemisphere.
If I rage any hotter,
I'll set even the memory of this room
ablaze.

*Let me go!* the stranger wails, the sound like a fist
on the inside of his coffin.
      (Wherever it is.)
*I know she's my wife!*
*I know it!*
*Let me dance with her!*
*Let me be with her!*

The circle of my hand
SNAPS
shut around the stranger's
and I draw back my other arm.
With enough force behind me,
I could knock this man's spirit
across the desolate sky if I wanted.

And I *do* want to.
I have to protect Renee, the way I failed to
in the sunlit world.

It's what we do
for the people we love—
we fight . . . for them.

**It's Virgil who seizes my fist**
in midstrike.
His own hand
      (the fingers bent into new shapes—
        treble clefs, half steps, grace notes)
is stronger than it should be.

The dead boy's embrace
is three-quarters concern, one-quarter frustration
as he says,
*Let this go.*
His words aren't orders or pleas,
but some combination
of the two.
*This man's grieving; he's confused.*
*Don't hurt him any more*
*than he's already been hurt.*
*We'll get him to listen*
*some other way.*

The stranger's pallid face
engulfs my vision and I struggle
to wrench myself free
of Virgil.
But as our guide
crushes me to his chest, my shirtsleeve
creeps,

one
        inch
               at a time,
up to my elbow.

It reveals
the eclipse inside me,
how it has spiraled to my shoulder,
painting me black.

Ariel has a song for this.
       (Rolling Stones, 1966.)
But it's muted
by the blood humming in my ears,
the fear that grabs me by the throat.
I fall back, my hip colliding
with the bar's sharp corner.
Yet I still manage to seethe
at the stranger,
*Stay away from Renee!*

My girlfriend isn't helpless though.
(I should have remembered that.)
She raises her camera like a torch.
The sight of it
commands me, Virgil, the stranger—
and so does the photo
Renee snaps.

The picture
travels into the stranger's waiting hands,
as if it knew
it was intended for him.

*Look at yourself in this picture,*
*then look at me*, Renee says to him.
*I can't be your family, some lost loved one.*
*Our spirits*
*don't look alike.*

The man's eyes drop to the photo.
As he takes in
his slim white form, his jagged contours,
his expression crumples
like the edges of the picture.
The apology he ushers out
rends at the air.
*I . . . I'm sorry.*
*I thought I knew you.*
*I thought you were someone*
*like* me.

Shoulders caving,
the man slouches away, taking his sadness
with him.

**Virgil brushes himself off.**
His sharpened gaze won't leave my arm—
and the black stars
studding its length.

I roll down my sleeve.
>                 (Too little, too late.)
*I'm sorry*, I say—
not to him, but to Renee.
>                 (I don't owe Virgil anything
>                 for unmasking me.)

*I'm not upset, Andres.*
*You were defending me*, Renee replies.
She wears the same look
>                 (shell-shocked, love-shocked)
she did after I thanked her
for pulling me back from the Yara lights.
Like she's struggling to swallow
what I've given her—
no matter how sweet it is.

Exhaling, Renee rolls on.
*Not a lot of people*
*have fought for me in the past.*
*Even* you *didn't,*
*when those boys bothered us*
*at Vizcaya.*
*I don't mind you being angry*
*on my behalf.*
*The trick is to know when to stop.*

I blink through the perpetual smoke
cloaking the theater.
*When to stop?*

Virgil pulls at my shirtsleeve
before I can banish him with a curse—
or an elbow to the ribs.
*When to know*
*you've gone* too *far.*
*Something*
*you* obviously *need to learn.*

Renee's curiosity is gentler.
Her hand drifts onto my knuckles.
       It's too close to my black stars
for comfort.
*Andres, about your arm. . . .*

But my own darkness means nothing
as the house lights
switch
off.

# CHAPTER
## THIRTY

**Burying all thoughts of my black stars,**
Renee and I scramble to find each other
so we won't be separated.

> (Like Liora was separated
> from *us*.)

But as the light returns,
one beam, one fractal, one molecule
at a time,
it's Liora Rose
who dominates the theater, the stage,
the tired ghosts who wail and cry
in jubilation.

Because it's *Liora* who radiates that light
from every strand of her hair,
the waves of her dress,

> (the lost river reborn)

the string of pearls,
        (knotted
        around her wrists like shackles)
the note she exhales
as she begins to sing.

**The dead flowers on each table**
erupt in living glory,
restored to purest white and passion red.
Liora's voice has raised them from decay,
rot, soil, memory.

The City dwellers
breathe in their fragrances,
and a hundred imitation heartbeats
flutter in sync with Liora's song.
The cracks in the theater's walls
stitch themselves closed;
the burn scars on the curtains
fold in on themselves.

Liora really is the muse of van Gogh, the City . . .
and perhaps the Prince too.

Our girlfriend kicks off her heels and twirls,
barefoot,
to the edge of the stage.
        (Some things don't change
        from one world to the next.)

The audience members reach for her,
drowning sailors
trying to bind themselves
to driftwood and rocky shores.
Liora skims her fingers over theirs,
making them sigh.

But our girlfriend isn't smiling.
Her eyes are silver mirrors,
reflecting
the ruins of the theater, the next turn of her heel,
the moment preceding it.

Liora is crystalline beauty,
untouched by the relief, the joy, the pain
of those around her.

And that isn't the Liora
I know.
That isn't the Liora
I fell in love with.

**Liora's cool strangeness**
doesn't change how badly
I want to sprint forward and take her
in my arms.
But I can't move.
Too many bodies hem me in,
and Renee's become a statue of a girl,
frozen in place.

This is
our best-case scenario . . . and our worst.

*She's your girlfriend then?* Virgil asks us.

*Yes*, Renee and I whisper,
together in all things.
           (More so down here
           than ever before.)

The dead boy
shakes his fire-branded head.
*God.*
*God, what a grave*
*you two have dug*
*with your own personal Beatrice.*

# CHAPTER
## THIRTY-ONE

**Beatrice, the girl who marched**
through the gates of Heaven
on Dante's behalf,
wasn't a real girl.

She was a *vision* of a girl, a story
repeated enough times to make her come alive
on the page.
But outside the lines of his poetry
and the circles of Hell he created,
Dante met the *real* Beatrice
twice.

He never kissed sugar from her mouth,
never laid his head in her lap,
never told her a secret or listened to her own
in exchange.

For Dante,
Beatrice was an *idea*,
the object of a quest
who was already tucked in her coffin
long before he picked up his pen.

But Liora's much more to us.

**Renee tugs on Ariel's strap, liberating my guitar**
from my shoulder.
*Andres, you have to play!* she says,
breaking from her trace.
*Liora will know your music, know* us,
*if you play!*

Can I make myself heard
above the din of the gray souls?

I have to try.

As I position my fingers
on Ariel's strings,
I let my love
be my guiding light.

My song isn't soft.
            (Love isn't, sometimes.)
It's a shout, a call to arms.
*See me, hear me, know me!* I cry.

*Beatrice, Beatrice,*
*our lady of summer days,*
*our lady of cotton candy smiles,*
*our lady of moments that feel like home.*

My music
crashes into Liora's melancholia.
If her song is the Yara lights, all illusion and glamour,
mine is the road under our feet,
intended to steady us.
If her song is the free fall of space,
mine is the transmission
meant to guide her back to earth.

But it's not recognition
reshaping Liora's features as she listens.
She's no longer a sheet of music;
she looks more like her mother
            (ice white and just as cold)
than the daughter
I poured into this song.

What I don't understand
is *why*.

**The crowd pulls back like the stage's curtain,**
making way for me and Renee,
Ariel and the song we've stitched together.
We're not City royalty . . .
but we *are* curiosities:

Renee vaults onto the stage, tripping
over her heels
in her haste to pull Liora into a kiss.
Half the audience hollers with approval.
        (If they can't have passion themselves,
        let them feast on someone else's.)
The other half spits in anger
as Liora's song peters out
against Renee's mouth.

I leap up beside my girlfriends,
my fingers rambling on my guitar strings
to create a new bridge.

*Liora!* I cry.
*We've come to bring you*
*home!*

# CHAPTER
## THIRTY-TWO

**Liora reels backward, taking my song**
with her.
Even the light of her dress
retreats from Renee and me.
*I don't know either of you!* Liora cries.
*I've never seen you two before!*

Pain flickers in me,
transforming my hands and heart
into embers.
           (Again.)
*Liora, please!* I beg.
*You* do *know us.*

The steps Renee takes toward Liora
are suddenly tentative—steps taken in a nightmare

where everything

        moves

                  too

     slowly.

*Andres is telling the truth*, she says.

*You've kissed us, loved us,*

*lived your life* with *us!*


Liora repeats her awful refrain.

*I don't remember you!*

*We've never met.*

*You must have mistaken me*

*for someone else.*

# CHAPTER
## THIRTY-THREE

**Every true ruler**
knows how to make a proper entrance.
Every would-be king
arrives with an entourage, wielding his forces
like swords.

The young man who strides onto the stage
has learned these lessons well.
He needs no introduction;
the dead give him one anyway.
*The Prince,*
*the Prince,*
*the Prince in the dark*, they whisper.

His title circles the theater—
like a buzzard about to settle on bones,
like the vulture men
who station themselves at the theater's doors.

They are
his soldiers, his bodyguards, his acolytes,
their heads bowed in worship silence.

The Prince in the dark
is tall and skeleton lean.
He hides his face
beneath the cascading hood of the cloak
lashing
at his heels like the animal I suspect
he is.
He's young; his hands
          (sun-soaked bronze
          despite the City's gloom)
aren't withered,
his spine isn't bent.

I don't want to recognize the way
the Prince holds himself.
I don't want to know
the machete-sharp angle his jaw curves at.

I don't want anything of his.
But it's too late for ignorance.
In one glance, I've already seen
too much.
And if the Prince peels back his hood,
so will everyone else.

          (But he doesn't reveal his face.
                  Not *yet*.)

**We, the living and the dead, are transfixed**
by the Prince's terrible grace.

The audience swoons
as he pulls soul after soul onto the stage,
granting his chosen few
a deep-throated kiss.
He drinks from their lips
like they did from the River Lethe,
and the dead go from autumn to winter
as he eats up their histories.

The Prince leaves the City's residents
bleeding
the same clean white light as Liora,
            (no memories to give them color)
and they end the kiss with a smile.
Oblivion *is* peace—
to them, at least.

Virgil is the sole spirit
who hasn't come forward
to offer the Prince his memories.
He stays at the bar,
his defiance
much quieter than the roar of his colors . . .
but no less firm for it.
He wants to *keep* his life.

            (Would I, if I had the choice?)

**The Prince grants seven kisses**
before his interest fades, leaving the audience
still clawing at his boots.
He crooks his finger
at Renee instead and purrs,
*And you?*
*Don't you want to forget?*

Renee stands on her toes
so she can meet the darkness
where the Prince's face should be.
But she stays at my side;
she must know this endless night-turned-boy
might steal her away
if she gives him an inch.

*What I want*
*is to return to the living world*, Renee snaps.
*What I want*
*is for you to return Liora's stolen memories*
*and let*
> *her*
>> *go.*

The Prince cackles.
*I didn't steal anything.*
*Liora gave me her memories—*
*didn't you?*

He pivots to Liora,
whose answer is in the white light around her . . .
and how it diminishes
the longer Renee and I stare at her.

Liora's husky whisper
is insistent as a scream.
*The Prince gave me what I wanted:*
*today but not yesterday or tomorrow.*
*And I give him what he wants:*
*beautiful things that bloom and grow*
*whenever I sing.*
*Fair is fair.*
*I didn't want to remember my past—*
*whatever it was.*
*And I still don't.*

I compose a clumsy fistful of notes
on Ariel's strings.
My guitar somehow makes them sweeter.
            (I can always count on her
            for that.)

*Come back*, I sing to Liora Rose.
*Ground Control*
*to Major Tom.*
*We'll trust you, if you trust us.*
*We won't look back; we'll be stronger*
*than the heroes who came before us*
*as we lead you*
*back to the world.*

*Please, Liora!*

The Prince laughs again;
the vulture men accompany him,
a rotten chorus
filling every doorway and corner of the theater.
Then he grazes
the nape of my neck with a slim finger,
sending a shiver
through every scrap of me.
*Liora has*
*what she wants*, the Prince tells me and Renee.

> *And it*
>
> *isn't*
>
> > *either of* you.

Petulance sours his regality,
adding a drop of childish lemon to it.
But childish or not, I should have brought a sword
to use against this boy
in place of a song.

Ariel will have to do.
I raise her above my head;
I raise my voice above the crowd,
intending to send both crashing down
on the Prince.

> (Sharp strings and minor seventh chords
> are good for that.)

But Liora
throws herself in front of him,
her arms spread to shield him.
*Please, stop!* she cries.

And

      I

                do.

*I want to stay!* Liora tells Renee and me.
*If the two of you love me*
*—whoever you are—*
*let me go.*
*Let me do*
*what makes me happy.*
*And this . . .*
Liora traces her lips
and the kiss
the Prince must have poisoned her with.
*This makes me happy.*

*And there*

      *you*

              *have it,*
crows the Prince.
*She's chosen me—*
*and not either of you!*
He hooks a hand on Liora's hip
and the vulture men
stream forward to surround them,
possessive and protective.

*Do you love the Prince,*
*whoever he really is?* Renee asks Liora,
reaching for a hand
she knows
she won't be able to clasp.

Captured in a moment she can't name,
a present with no past behind it,
Liora says,
*He's all I remember.*
*And that's enough.*

**We could follow Liora; we could chase her**
to the end of this ever-dying world
and whatever rambles beyond it.
But we buckle
under the pain
and let Liora disappear—
through the curtains, the gilded doors, and into
the unknown—without us.

I can't force myself to move;
my feet are stone, just another wing
of this crumbling theater.
And Renee's are no different.

The rain here washes everything away:
civilizations, music, hope.
Renee's fire?
It's another causality.

*I knew it*, she whispers.
*I knew Liora would throw me away*
*eventually.*

This is all
my
fault.

# CANTO III
## THE PRINCE
## IN THE DARK

# CHAPTER
## THIRTY-FOUR

**The show is over;**
its clockwork ballerina and her Prince
have made their exit.

Soul by soul, the people of the City
leave the theater, their eyes damp with regret . . .
or gratitude.
It makes no difference to me.

Renee and I are two flakes of ash,
barely human.
With nowhere else to go, we flit backstage.
(Because grief
has no final destination.)

It's Virgil who discovers us
cocooned in the smoke-choked curtains.

How much time has passed
since Liora and the Prince left?
How long ago
did our sorrow begin?
I can't even begin to guess.

*I told you*
*the singing girl belongs to the Prince.*
Virgil's voice
is as heavy with resignation
as the streets are
with the weight of spirits.
*Come on, you two.*
*Let's get out of here.*

Renee ushers her question
through lips that must be numb.
        (Like mine.)
*Where*
*are you taking us now?*

Virgil extends his hands
and a fragile thread of hope.
*Some place better than this;*
*some place where you can think*
*about what you want to do*
*next.*
Then he reminds us,
*It's not over*
*until* you *decide it is.*

**Our trio**
        (two lost kids and a dead boy,
        the start of some terrible joke)
escapes the ruined theater,
shaking curls of smoke from our clothes
as we go.
But me and Renee's sense of loss
doesn't disappear as easily; we'll wear it
for a long time to come.

The three of us speed past
the Library of Alexandria,
various incarnations of London, Tokyo, and Chicago
razed by bombs and fires.

Virgil ignores these monuments,
steering us
to a filing cabinet of a building
nestled against the City's bone wall.
The chipped walls and splintered windows
tell stories
in a language I can't quite make out.

*It's dry inside*, Virgil offers.
*And quiet.*

There's nothing welcoming
about this building;
no one comes and goes through the doors
suspended on their fragile hinges.

But the rain cuts like a knife;
we need to take shelter.

I hold out the crook of my elbow
for Renee—
a false gentleman for a lady
I may not deserve.
*Shall we?* I ask.

Renee twines our arms together.
Despite what she saw in the theater,
she's still willing to touch me.

                  (For now.)

**We climb staircase after staircase,**
seven in all.
The air aches with silence,
the way my lungs do
as we reach the final landing.

*Sorry about all the steps*, says Virgil.
*There was an elevator, once.*
*But we lost power*
*early in the war;*
*I can't remember*
*what the building was like,*
*lit up and electric.*

*What* was *this place?* Renee asks him.
*What makes it important enough*
*to be carried here,*
*moment by moment, brick by brick?*

Virgil scrapes his knuckles
on the nearest doorframe.
(For luck, maybe.)
*It was my home*, he replies.
*That makes it more important*
*than any other building.*
*To* me, *anyway.*

I nod, breathing in
snow gone silver with ash,
the illusion of steaming tea and beet soup.

For a boy made of torn muscles,
Virgil outraces us easily to the last door
on the right.
It's no different
from any others we've passed,
but he jostles the lock open, bouncing
almost merrily over the threshold.

*Welcome*
*to my apartment*, Virgil announces.

**Virgil's tour of his home is brief.**
He points out:
a kitchen narrow as a needle,
a bedroom shared by too many boys,
        (socks and soccer balls
        creating new landmarks
        on the floor)
a window overlooking a swing set
overgrown with vines,
empty flats
that should have been filled with fellow souls,
        laughing,
        quarreling,
        dancing.
This apartment is a relic, but I suspect
it was loved.

*Were you happy here?* I ask Virgil.

*The happiest*, he replies.
*It doesn't look like much.*
*It* wasn't *much, truth be told.*
*But this is where I lived*
*all my best moments.*

**A pudgy boy, his hair dark as a forgotten corner,**
streaks past us.
He moves like Liora, in time with secret music;
a giddy brass band
must be playing inside him.

Renee and I step quickly aside to make way
for his enthusiasm.
The little boy
darts through us, sending our clothes
rippling in his wake.

Renee follows him with her gaze
as he fades into the bedroom.
A second later,
the boy runs past us again,
his laughter ricocheting off the walls
in a joyous loop.
*Who is that, Virgil?* she says.
*Does another soul*
*stay here with you?*

Virgil can't keep his eyes
off the boy either.
*No; I'm by myself.*
*But memory*
*can be livelier than anything*
*here in the City.*
*That kid's a memory of mine.*
His grin is too fierce,
like he's fighting back
a sob.
*He was*
            (*he* is, *somewhere*)
*my little brother.*

Renee shifts away
from Virgil's ghost-of-a-ghost.
*Why bring the echo of him here,*
*along with your home?*
*Isn't it more painful to see him*
*than to let the memory of him*
*go?*

For one
        terrible
                minute,
Virgil's hair
fades to the same shade
as the tea-colored wallpaper.
*Neither of you has siblings—*
*I*
        *can*
*tell,* he says.
*You're not always looking behind you;*
*you're not always waiting*
*for someone else's footsteps to catch up*
*with your own.*
*But I can barely remember a time*
*when my brother wasn't with me.*
*So silence*
*just feels wrong now.*

I put a hand on Virgil's shoulder,
mindful of the bone shards.
*Your brother survived; you didn't.*

*But you both lived*
*in this building.*
*What happened?*

Virgil melts against me
and the window's splintered remains,
like the snow outside
never will.
For Virgil and this building, it will always be
March 2022, and the war
will always soldier on.
*I heard the rocket*
*before it hit our flat.*
*I pushed my brother*
*out of the way, out of the kitchen, into the hall.*
*Love doesn't mean abandoning yourself*
*to make somebody else happy.*
*Love means being willing*
*to be your* truest *self.*
*I didn't realize*
*who my true self was*
*until I was faced with a choice:*
*me or my brother, his life or mine.*
*I chose.*
Our guide inspects his raw knuckles—
a clever way to avoid
our eyes.
*Don't get me wrong;*
*my true self wasn't a hero.*
*But I guess he had a lot of love*
*to give.*

# CHAPTER
## THIRTY-FIVE

**Virgil leaves us to the privacy of our grief**
in his battered living room.
And we leave him to his.

I stroke Ariel's strings, attempting to gather
the last of my courage and my songs.
But I'm not sure I have enough of either
to carry us
any farther than this room.

*What do we do now?*
I hate to ask Renee this;
I hate to put even more on her shoulders
when it's only because of her wisdom
that we've come this far.

Renee folds herself up
on the plastic-wrapped couch,
its yellow flowers too cheerful
for my current taste.

*I made myself believe*
*this journey would get easier*
*once we found Liora,* Renee says.
*That we could lead her out of the City*
*if only we didn't*
*look back, eat the pomegranate,*
*taunt the sinners.*
*I made myself believe*
*Eurydice wouldn't reject her rescuers.*
*But none of that was true.*
*We failed; I failed.*

*We haven't failed yet,* I try,
but the words rattle, uncertain,
in my mouth.

Renee's camera
            (dim now)
clatters against her breastbone
as she pulls her knees to her chest.
*What do you suggest we do, Andres?*
*Go to this Prince*
*in the dark?*
*Pay him an obol coin*
*for Liora's safe passage?*

*Beat him at a game of chess*
*beside the colorless sea?*
She laughs, the sound hollow.
*The myths were all wrong.*
*Persephone ate her pomegranates* willingly.
*She left us, Andres.*
*She doesn't want to go home.*
*She doesn't want* us.

I raise a hand
dripping with darkness.
*I don't think that's true.*
*It's* my *fault*
*Liora went with the Prince.*
*I frightened her—*
*with my frustration and my temper.*
(I can confess that much . . . but no more.)

*It wasn't you that frightened her;*
*this City is a* place *of fear*, Renee replies.
*Regrets gather here*
*like crows on a carcass.*
*Whatever you fear*
*is going to find you.*
She dips
her head and voice low.
*It's already found me.*

And me too.
But I can't let Renee know that.

**Virgil, not much for solitude,**
saunters back to the couch.
Behind him, I hear
small feet darting down the hall,
the furious whistle of rockets, the ballad of his life.
(Ended, but still echoing.)

*Well?* Virgil asks us,
propping
what's left of his shoulder on the doorframe.
*Will you stay*
*in the City to find your true love,*
*or will you go back to the sun?*

I twist my shadow-scarred hands.
*What would you do, Virgil?*
*You've seen what we're up against;*
*you've seen how pointless*
*our journey might be.*

Virgil rocks forward, a sunflower
straining for the warmth of the world.
*I'm dead.*
*I don't get an opinion*
*on how you spend your life.*
*But.*

Renee and I lean forward
on the memory of this boy's couch.
*But . . . ?*

*But I know love*, says Virgil.
*I know how it can run through your hands*
*like sand,*
*like time you only* think *you have.*
*If I could do it all again,*
*I'd always chase after what I loved.*
*Even if*
              (*even* when)
*it led me to danger.*

*Isn't that*
*how you died?* I say.

There's no humor in Virgil's laugh;
only hard-won truth.
*It is.*
*But like I said before,*
*I accept the choice I made.*
*If the two of you leave now,*
*will* you *regret it?*

The answer we share
comes on like a storm—
fierce and immediate.
*Yes*, we say.

And in that *yes*,
we find our own answer.

Liora may not want me as I am;
she may not want us as *we* are.
But she deserves better
than the Prince
who keeps her locked inside his kiss.

**Renee pries herself off the couch.**
I let her help me up; I let myself lean on her.
We're getting better
at coming as we are—
tired or weak, hopeless or hopeful.

*Do you know*
*where the Prince*
*in the dark lives?* Renee asks Virgil.

*Not exactly*, he says.
*But it won't be too hard to find him.*
*All we have to do is look*
*for the place*
*where whatever light's still here*
*goes to die.*

I raise my brows
gray sky-high.
"We"?
*I thought you said*
*you wouldn't go any farther with us.*

Virgil shrugs, his favorite gesture
by far.
*What I can say?*
*I'm invested*
*in how this ends for the two of you*
*and the singing girl.*
*I want to see*
*how far love will*

       (*how far love* can)

*take you.*


**Virgil doesn't lock the door**
to his phantom flat.

       (*There was nothing to steal*
       *when it was in the living world.*
       *There's even less to steal now,* he tell us.
       *Who wants a memory*
       *that isn't even theirs?*)
He knocks on the banisters as we go,
treating every touch
like a goodbye.


Does Virgil know something
we don't?
Or does he do this every time he leaves
out of loyalty,
a promise to return?


If I could make my wish
come true,

if Renee and Liora and I could grow up
      (and grow old)
in a home of our own, would I love that building
as much as Virgil loves this one?
Would I treat every cramped room
like a shrine?

*One day,*
*we'll have this,* I murmur to Renee.
*A place we don't just exist in,*
*but a place where we can be ourselves.*
Maybe I'm channeling Liora
      (or the way she used to be),
divining a future too optimistic
to be real.
But as I press this vow to the shell of Renee's ear
as I've pressed kisses
so many times before, it feels like it *could* be real.
Like it could *ours*.

> If we ever find our way
> home from these silver streets
> soaked with the tears
> of millions across history.
> If we ever find our way
> out of the labyrinth
> my past has trapped us in.

> I have to make this right—
> no matter what.

# CHAPTER
## THIRTY-SIX

**No one is alone in the City for long.**
There's always someone
hunched on a corner,
hovering under a gas lamp,
lingering in a doorway, unable to decide
whether to stay or to go on.

There's always someone
*seeking*.
Our trio seeks the dying light . . .
and the vulture men
seek the three of *us*.

They appear
in the yawning mouths of alleyways,
beneath guttering neon signs,
on the thresholds of crumbling buildings.

*Keep walking*, Virgil instructs us.
*Predators smell fear*
*faster than anything.*

It's good advice.
But in life,
the vulture men were loyal to no one
except themselves.
In death
their alliance is different;
they belong to the Prince
and all his desires.
His kiss
must let them forget
how they spent their time on earth.
Even the wicked have a conscience;
it chases us all down, one way
or another.

And it's the vulture men
who chase *us* now.
They glide, stomp, march up to us,
showing off
their gnashing teeth and broken grins.
*You're not to go near*
*the Prince's singer!* his army barks,
a single grasping, tearing mass.
They grab
at our wrists and hair,
the strap of Renee's camera, Ariel's strings.

Their collective touches are unbearable
as they pull
our group apart.
One man grips my shoulder,
another grinds callused knuckles
into my cheek.
His skin hums with radioactivity—
he dropped bombs
and enjoyed the afterburn.

The feel of these men
brings me back to—
my hands clamped over my ears,
locking out
the tidal crash of my parents' arguments;
Eduardo's shirt knotted in my fists,
the crack of his jaw as I silenced him;
a future that's just the past
in different, shabbier clothing.

You can't escape yourself,
especially here in the City,
and the proof of that
is in the shadows on my arms.
They hunt
for the glowing places in me,
trying to snuff them out . . . for good.

But.
*But.*

Wasn't I more
than this, above
if not below?
Didn't I have more love
than darkness to give
when I lived beside the mermaid girls?

I failed
to save Liora from my own selfishness.
I can't fail
to save her now.

**I fight for Ariel; she hurls herself into my hands.**
I find her strings by sense memory, *soul* memory.
I find her music using the same.

*Ground Control*
*to Major Tom*, I call
to myself, to Renee and Virgil,
strumming all the right chords.
      (Ariel knows the way through this,
      even if I don't.)
*We're more*
*than these monsters*
*and the shadows they paint us with.*
*We don't need to be afraid*
*of what they show us.*
*But they should be afraid*
*of what we can show them.*

The brilliance in Renee's eyes
sputters back to life.
She drives a sharp elbow deep
into the ribs
of the nearest vulture man,
and brings her thumb down
on her camera's shutter.

As she does, photos of the vulture men
       (and all their memories)
start to dance
in the rain.

# CHAPTER
## THIRTY-SEVEN

**The vulture men recoil;**
they must fear being exposed
more than I did.
(Than I still *do*.)

I can't blame them.
Their histories don't appear
in bursts of circus tones, soft golds, roiling summer blues.
The pictures of their memories
are rust-colored images
of gardens grown from secrets,
basements built for bloodlettings,
an existence
picked clean of love, family, friendship.

The vulture men cover their eyes,
hiding from the light of Renee's camera
and the truth.

They don't want to see
their own emptiness, their corrosive lives on earth.
      (They haven't had a bright thought
        in years, have they?)

**But it's our own bright thoughts that will save us.**
I strike another chord and say,
*Ground Control to Major Tom—*
the closet thing I have to a spell,
the only means I have to rescue anyone.

It's Virgil
I sing to now, my message clear
in any language—
English, Ukrainian, the tenor of the stars
we're all made of.

The dead boy nods,
and Renee aims her camera at him
for the first time.

He tells us,
*Outside Mariupol,*
*there are sunflower fields that go on*
*forever.*
*My friends and I*
*found shelter in them—*
*from school, arguments with our parents,*
*the long winters*
*skulking toward us*
*from the other side of September.*

In the photo Renee has taken,
a parade of boys
darts through the flowers,
laughing
as they kick a soccer ball back and forth.
Virgil (his face and life intact)
throws grins at his friends
like his countrymen will one day be forced
to throw grenades.

Virgil watches his old self, his troupe of ghosts.
*I can look at my past*
*without cowering,* our guide tells us.
*I can stay in the present*
*without losing myself.*
*Maybe I can even walk into a future*
*that's more than this place.*
He fires off a raging look
at the vulture men.
*Which is more than I say*
*for any of you.*

**The photos of Virgil's memories**
form an aurora.
They are the most extraordinary parts of life
surrounding the men who give us
its most terrible moments.

(The newspaper boy was right:
the best is yet to come.
The newspaper boy was right:
the worst is yet to come.)

Virgil isn't a flame contained
in a jar.
He becomes
a thousand miles of sunflowers
as he yells at the vulture men
and all their sins:
*I see you, FSB fascist assholes.*
*I see you, arms dealers, brother killers.*
*I see you sweatshop bosses, oil executives,*
*Wagner mercenaries.*
His ever-expanding grin is bigger than the City
and the sad imitation of life here.
*I see you and what you've done.*
*And none of it scares me.*
*But it clearly*

> *scares*

> > you.

**The vulture men can't stand us or themselves**
for one more instant.

They rush, river rapid, back to their hideaways
like the cowards they are—
the kind Renee, Virgil, and I
refuse to be.

But Virgil's light doesn't dissipate
with their departure.
It turns into a knife, splitting open
the air itself.

It's not a wound that appears
in the sky.
It's a door, a window, a *possibility*.
It's a way out,
opening onto roses, marigolds, an ending
I recognize.

This isn't Renee's and my exit.
            (Not today, anyway.)
This hole in the City's time and space
is for Virgil alone.

**The scarred boy blinks**
what's left of his hair from his single eye.
The other, lost in shrapnel, narrows.
The door's message
is clear:
*Embrace whatever comes next.*
*Or stay*
*in the painful familiar.*

*I wasn't expecting this*, Virgil confesses.
*I wasn't expecting to leave you*
*or the City*
*just yet.*

*But leaving*
*is the best thing for you.*
Renee lifts a photo
of Virgil's sunflowers from a puddle
it has lent its golden glow to.
*It's like you said—*
*you won't lose*
*your home, your brother, yourself*
*if you walk into the future.*

I clap a hand on Virgil's back,
brother to brother.
*Exactly.*
*The love you have*
*for all those things?*
*It's inside you.*
*And Renee's photos prove it.*
*They can only show*
*the truth—*
*ugly or radiant, damaged or whole.*

Virgil trails his fingers
over the flower petals and dark seeds
held captive in the picture.
The photo is already losing its luster;
the rain makes sure of *that*.

The dead boy's mouth breaks
into a grin,
like the gray sky has broken
for him.

*Well*, Virgil says.
*Whatever's on the other side*
*can't be worse*
*than this place.*

My own laughter
slices through the downpour—
a gate leading past despair,
the way all laughter is supposed to be.
*I think you're right.*

Virgil exhales his last breath
of City air
and gives Renee
what's left of the dissolving photograph.
But his final gift
is something else entirely.

*My real name*
*is Vasyl,* he tells us.
*Now you can remember me*
*the way I really am.*

Then Virgil-Vasyl, the boy who loved,
steps through the window
      and

          is

               gone.

There will be other boys
from Mariupol, Kyiv, Aleppo
who cross that same threshold.
There will be other boys
from other wars
who will vanish from our world and enter
the next.

But there could also be peace for them
on the other side.

# CHAPTER
## THIRTY-EIGHT

**The City feels emptier without Virgil at our side,**
cracking jokes like the thunder.

*I'm glad he left*, I say to Renee
as we trudge on, lashed by wind and rain.
*But I'll miss him.*

Renee loops her arm through mine,
a thread trying to stitch up
the hole Virgil left in his wake.
*I will too.*
*He was braver than most people—*
*living or dead.*

As we walk,
the rain and the glow of the lampposts
begin to fade, and the crooked street
finally ends—
but not at the wall encircling the City.

Virgil told us
the Prince lives
in the part of the City
where the light goes to die.
And the abyss
yawning open at our feet is just that.

The Prince must be
on the other side . . .
but there's no telling how far down
the pit goes.
If Renee and I fall into it,
we might never stop.
We might hover in this void
        *(Ground Control*
        *to Major Tom)*
until our bodies crumble somewhere above,
just pillars of salt and sand.

I kick at the pavement.
        (It doesn't yield to me.)
*How can we cross this?* I demand,
of the abyss, the universe, Death herself.
*There's no bridge, no way to get past it!*

*Our peacock and jaguar!* Renee reminds me.
*They told us we could summon them*
*one last time*
*if we needed a road*
*where there wasn't one.*
*Play something, Andres!*
*Play something to call them.*

**The song for Renee's peacock comes to me easily.**
It's the puckish sound of dawn
cresting over the sea.

The song for my jaguar is more of a challenge.
It's four-note melody,
an ominous approach, a long-held breath.

But each song is true; each song is powerful.
My music peels back the rain,
        (just for a moment)
creating
a window to the (dead) woods,
where the peacock and the jaguar
glimmer and snarl.
They step into the City to join us,
grace and something far more lethal.

I point to the abyss.
*We need help*, I say.
*We need a road forward.*

The jaguar thrashes her tail
on the ground.
It's an act of annoyance,
not anger.

> (I used to drum my fingers the same way
> on desks, car doors, some other boy's cheek
> as I considered
> whether he was worth hitting
> or not.)

*To find a road*
*out of the abyss, you must* enter *it.*
*You must*
*go deeper.*


Renee moves to the pit's edge,
the tips of her boots
suspended
in the air.
She's borrowed the pose from Liora.

> (We need to keep our girlfriend here with us
> *somehow.)*

*Of course.*
*You have to hit rock bottom*
*before you can climb*
*up to something better.*


I don't like the weariness in her tone,
like she's already struck hard ground
after a fall.

(But did it happen in the burned-out theater . . .
or in the living world?)

Renee holds her camera
over the abyss.
A burst of light follows, and a photograph
lands at our feet, a revelation
of what we're about to face.

The abyss isn't empty;
I should have remembered darkness
never is.
There's always something
gazing back at you.
And what gazes back at *us*
is an ocean
of scorpions.

The heat of my temper
stirs in my chest as I round on my jaguar.
Her eyes are as impartial
as stones that have seen the beginning
and end of history.
She may think nothing of this—
but I do.

*We can't go down there!* I shout.
*The scorpions—*

*Will not sting you*, the peacock interrupts,
*if you go deeper.*

Renee's desperate serenity doesn't fray
at the edges;
it splinters like Liora did
in the car wreck.
*Please, we don't understand.*
*What do you mean?*

The jaguar pads to my side,
but her weight isn't a comfort; it's a reminder
of what we are.
*You will*, says the jaguar.
*Or you won't.*
*The pain you suffer*
*will be decided by you.*
*Not us.*
*Not even the scorpions.*
*They only give*
*what is given to* them.

Every answer is a riddle
I can't solve.
But—

Renee finishes the thought.
*But we've come too far to turn back*
*now.*

# CHAPTER
## THIRTY-NINE

**How do you find your lowest point?**
You give up; you give in.
You let go.

Renee and I link arms.
(Misery loves company.)

Silent as screams
trapped behind a picture frame,
we tip
over the edge of the abyss.

We let ourselves
fall.

Gravity works, even here
where reality's an extended game of pretend.

We aren't meteors; we don't make impact.
We fly, as souls must.

**The scorpions**
          (a hundred, a thousand, *more*)
don't swarm us in the pit.
They're more thoughtful with their cruelty.
The amble up
our legs, bodies, outstretched arms,
contemplating
where to plunge their stingers.

I'm foolish enough to think
maybe they won't harm us;
maybe they'll have mercy.
We didn't come here for glory
but for love.
Isn't that worthy
of a little kindness?

And that's when the first stinger
                    STABS
my hand.
And the next.
And the next.

I scream, shock and pain
coating my throat.
(The taste is coffee bitter.)

I fall back—and as I do, the scorpions go still
as the snow
I've never seen.

*If we stop,*
*the scorpions do too*, I gasp.
*If we stay where we are,*
*they won't hurt us.*

But Renee is already ahead of me.
*We* can't *stop!* she calls.
Her hand, hibiscus red and swollen, twitches
at her side.
I want to take it.
(I know I can't.)
*We have to go forward.*
*We have to go—*

*Deeper*, my jaguar cuts in.
*You must go deeper.*

**The peacock and the jaguar**
take up a chant.

> *Go.*
> *Deeper.*
> *Go.*
> *Deeper.*

The scorpions
drive their poison into me and Renee,
relentless.
I swear in three languages;
Renee's cries bob in her throat, messages
in a bottle
she won't allow to reach her lips.
*It's just pain*, she reminds us both.
*It fades eventually.*

*No*, I say.
*It's more than that.*
*It's* me *seeing* you
*in pain.*
*It's you seeing the same thing*
*with me.*

It would be different
if either of us were alone.
If all we had to endure were the (endless)
        prick,
        prick,
        prick
of stingers.

But we have to witness
the scorpions skitter over our lover
and be unable to swat them away.

We have to watch them
strike
again and again,
and chart the course of blood
as it runs from skin we've brushed tenderly.
And isn't *that* the worst pain of all?

The jaguar bares her teeth
in a smile.
*Deeper*, she urges.
*You're almost there.*

I want to believe her.
But the other side of the abyss
seems a century away, a hundred long years of suffering
I can't carry for Renee
and she can't shoulder for me.

Even Ariel feels heavier with every step
I take,
a mountain
flattened against the arch of my spine.
The scorpions attack her too,
but as they skitter up her bridge,
all their stingers evoke
are a few notes from her steel strings.
Their song is a taunt.
          (*Go deeper.*)
Ariel's refrain is an answer.
               (*Inside* yourself.)

**Odysseus, silver-tongued as I used to be,**
didn't travel to the underworld
to join the dead.
He was seeking knowledge to lead him
home—
to love, to his wife, to the sanctuary
he could only find in both.

But when he descended,
what he found first
was his own grief, his losses laid bare;
his dead brothers-in-arms, his mother,
the years he'd never get back.
In the underworld, in death,
Odysseus found the truth—
ugly as it was.

To show Renee my black stars
is one thing;
to confess I may be the cause
of every moment of despair
she's felt since we arrived here
is another.
But what if that's the only way
to save Liora?

The scorpions wait
for me to make my choice.
Will I lose my lovers
or lose their love for *me*?

Will I hide
behind the safety of my shadows
or step into the glaring light?

Will I be like the Prince,
a black hole of selfishness?
Or will I be more like Virgil,
sel*fless* in the end?

*Renee!* I shout. *Wait.*

**The terrible wisdom I'm forced to share:**
*Renee, listen to me.*
*Distance here isn't measured*
*in only kilometers or miles.*
*It's measured*
*in what we think, what we feel.*
*What's in the deepest part of us?*
*The* hidden *part of us?*
*A wound, a moment*
*when we were trapped in some other abyss*
*just as real as this one.*

Renee takes on the aspect of my jaguar,
her teeth flashing
in a snarl.
*If I wanted to talk about my wounds,*
*I would have already!*

*I don't want you to know all of mine*
*either*, I admit.
*But I don't want to see you in pain*
*even more.*

Renee's stance begins to soften.
Everyone, everywhere
dons heavy armor to move through the world.
(*Any* world.)
But slowly, she peels her own off,
like it's grown too small
to contain her.

*Deeper*, Renee tells herself.
But the story that follows
is for me.

# CHAPTER
## FORTY

**In Miami, I told you what magic is**
*and isn't.*
*But you and Liora aren't the first people*
*I shared my magic with.*

Renee presses the shutter of her camera,
sending a photo, a *memory*
waltzing through the darkness.

In the picture, my girlfriend is younger,
her smile an invitation.
But there are lies
clouding the eyes of the friends
who wrap their arms around her.

*At first,*
*my old friends saw my magic*
*as interesting, special,* exotic, Renee says.

*They thought*
*it could give their life flavor—*
*a dash of garlic for protection,*
*a sprinkle of cinnamon for abundance.*
*They clamored for enchantment—*
*kids in a candy store, touching everything*
*with sticky fingers.*

*They wanted me to be*
*a fairy godmother, a good witch in frosting pink.*
*They reached and reached—*
*for more and more magic.*
*But whenever you reach*
*into the unknown, something else*

> *may*

> *reach*

> *back.*

*And that something*
*may have* teeth.
*I always warned my friends:*
*Never deal with any spirit*
*that won't give you its name;*
*never dream-walk into places*
*you don't know the way back from.*
*They refused to listen.*

The scorpions
on her arms and legs
halt.
But their barbs stay at the ready,
bright with venom.

The phoenix-girl
holds up her camera again,
snapping a photo of the abyss's depths.
The second picture
shows the same circle of friends
cowering
before specters, claws, Yara lights—
things they should have locked their doors
against.

The voices of those friends
swell in the air around us, rattling my bones—
and Renee's.

*This is* your *fault, Renee!*

*You're a freak!*
*You're a monster!*
*We're done with you!*

*Your world is dangerous!*
*You're* dangerous!

Renee continues above the accusations:
*Whenever my friends got hurt*
*by the unseen world,*
*they stopped seeing me as an ally*
*in love and war games*
*and started to see me as a threat.*

*As if I'd called the shadows*
*that followed them home*
*because they didn't think*
*to check behind them.*
*As if I was responsible*
*for keeping them safe*
*from themselves.*

*They wanted me to protect them.*
*And I'm no one's keeper.*
*I want to be with equals!*
*But they didn't respect me*
*or the magic*
*they had me teach them.*
*In their terror, they threw me away*
*and replaced me with safer friends,*
*powdered sugar sweet.*

Renee raises trembling fingers,
dashing away her tears.
The last photo she takes
is the worst of them all:
Renee's (former) friends turning from her,
barbed whispers on their lips.
And each whisper becomes a cut
my girlfriend slashes
on her own wrist.

**Renee is a nautilus shell,**
curling in on herself.
*I'm afraid*
*when we go home, you and Liora*
*will be scared of what I can do,*
*of how I brought you here—*
*even if you come back intact,*
*even if we save her.*
*I'm afraid*
*you'll want to return to the mundane,*
*the way people always do.*

I ask her,
*How long*
*have you been waiting*
*for Liora and I*
*to walk away from you,*
*like your old friends did?*

Renee's answer
scrapes us both raw.
*Since you and she*
*took your first steps*
*toward me.*
*And I was right to be afraid*
*you two would leave,*
*wasn't I?*
*Because in the end,*
*Liora did.*

The scorpions, satisfied
by her truth
(and the pain she's unearthed),
travel down Renee's arms and legs, forming a pool
at her ankles.

But there's still my truth
to deal with.

> Confession's supposed to be good for the soul.
> But I don't think what I have to say
> will be good
> for *anyone*.

**I'm happy to give this part of the truth away:**
*I'm not afraid of you, Renee.*
*Of your magic*
*or any other part of you.*
*You've only ever used your power*
*for good, for* love.

This part of the truth is harder to reveal:
*But you and Liora*
*might have been afraid of the boy*
*I used to be.*
*I was powerful too; I was also a brute.*
*I erupted, I screamed; I lashed out*
*at everyone*
*with my fists and dragon-fire words.*
*Back then, I knew*
*I was cruel.*

*And I wanted (so badly!) to be kinder.*

I hang my head snake-belly low.
Even without Ariel joining me,
my sorrow's a lullaby, putting the scorpions at ease.
*Everyone has a shadow side;*
*everyone has flaws, imperfections.*
*But my shadows were deep enough*
*to drown in.*

*Last year,*
*when I drowned for* real
          *(when I* died),
*I arrived in a field of flowers*
*where I met Death herself.*
*She returned me to the living world*
*and cut away*
*my pointless fury.*
*She cut away my* shadow.

Renee shifts to face me . . .
and what I've told her.
*What happened to your shadow,*
*after?*

My laugh is strangled.
*Where does Peter Pan's shadow go*
*when he loses it?*
*Where do all shadows go*
*when they're unwanted?*

*Down,*

      *down,*

            *into*

            *the underground.*

*I left my shadow* here, *Renee.*
*And it's coming to find me.*
*Just look at my arms!*
I rip my sleeve up, putting myself
on display.
*I'm terrified of my shadow.*
*But I'm even more afraid of the promise*
*I made Death:*
*to give her something I loved*
*in exchange for my liberation.*
My next words are broken glass; they cut me
as they roll off my tongue.
*What if* Liora *was what, was* who
*I sold*
*to Death?*


I wait to be abandoned, along with hope.


But my girlfriend blows out a sigh,
not a storm.
*I appreciate your honesty, Andres.*
*For what it's worth,*
*your past and your shadow*
*don't scare me.*
*Whoever you were before,*
*you're not that boy* now.

*You're not cruel; you're not violent.*
Renee's faint smile
combats the gloom.
*And I don't think Death is*
*either.*
*She's fair, over everything else.*

*Whatever Death's price was,*
*it couldn't have been Liora.*
*Because Liora's life was never yours*
*to give.*
*It belongs to* her—
*whatever she chooses to do with it,*
*whoever she chooses to spend it with.*

Relief crushes me into diamond dust
          and as I crumple to my knees,
the ground
levels out, becoming ribbon flat.

We've reached
the bottom of the abyss.
Now we have to find the strength
to rise.

**It's easier to crash**
than it is to find a way back
from your own personal apocalypse.
The same holds true for any climb.

The walls of the abyss aren't sheer,
but Renee and I still have to crawl
one aching step, one fistful of dirt
at a time.

*You are*
*so close*, our guides say.
*Just*

       *keep*

            *going.*

*So close*, Renee and I echo.

I take up more than this chorus though;
I take up new oaths
in place of arms.
*When we get back, when this is done,*
*we're going to buy*
*vanilla ice cream, white chocolate,*
*roses, and sparklers*, I tell Renee.
*We're going to celebrate with Liora—*
*every small victory, every day.*
*I promise, I promise, I promise.*

**We don't emerge from the abyss into sunlight**
or starshine.
Those things are ahead of us,
somewhere.
But we do emerge as *ourselves*.

**The peacock and the jaguar have retired,**
their work complete;
our path ahead is clear of guards and monsters.
But something else is waiting for us
beneath the gray sky.

Renee gasps, a girl with an apple
              (knowledge or poison?)
lodged in her throat.
*What is this?* she asks.
*Andres, what is this?*

What is it?
A little piece of home
in the wrong realm.

# CHAPTER
## FORTY-ONE

**The Versace Mansion**
　　　　(1116 Ocean Drive, Miami Beach)
was never burned or torn down
like the other buildings in the City.
But the mansion can't escape its two legacies:
splendor . . . and death.
Maybe that's why
it has a reflection of its own
under
kingdom come.

The mosaic pool in the mansion's courtyard
lit up in rainbow lights,
the rooms splashed with tropical colors,
the hidden doors
ready to show the wealthy and the beautiful
the secret heart of the house

all coexist
with the blood on the steps, the smell of gunfire
haunting the air.


In Miami, tourists photograph the gates
where the house's most famous owner
    (Gianni Versace, the prince of fashion)
was shot,
his hands full of newspapers,
his head full of a day that promised
to be ordinary.
(And wasn't.)


If the tourists were trying to be witches,
they were hacks
compared to Renee.
None of them
ever called on the memory of Mr. Versace
with their cameras.
He remained elsewhere.
I think he must be elsewhere, still.


Because in the land of the dead, the Versace Mansion
is framed by black lights.
And that means a very different prince
uses it as his lair.


        Secondary definition of a haunt:
          a place animals go to feed.

**The mansion's gates, woven from iron flowers,**
aren't locked;
when Renee tugs on one, it gives
easily.
*Too* easily.

Her fingers flying back from the lock,
Renee asks,
*Why aren't there guards here?*
*Dictators anywhere*
*are notoriously paranoid.*

I rub my palms together,
desperate to have my shadows retreat.
      (They don't.
      They circle
      my biceps, collar, the nape of my neck.)
*Not this dictator.*
*Princes are the thing in the story*
*everyone else should be afraid of.*

I stride
past the gates, Renee,
the echo of the gunshot that launched Versace's soul
out of one world, into the next.

*You know who he is, don't you?* Renee presses.
*This Prince in the dark.*

*I have an idea*, I admit,
*but no proof.*

Renee strums two dark chords
		(diminished E, diminished D)
on Ariel's strings.
*You don't need proof*
*to be afraid,* she says.
*You just need to see something awful*
*from the corner of your eye.*
*What did you see in the theater*
*that I didn't, Andres?*
*What did you see*
*in the Prince?*

I keep my back to her.
It's safer.
(Orpheus taught me that much.)
*Nothing.*
*And that's exactly*
*the problem.*

**The courtyard of the Versace Mansion**
is impossibly alive; the warm air blankets us
in false relief.
We aren't home . . .
but it's tempting to pretend
we are.

Sparkling dragonflies
perform ballets over our heads;
dune grass and red crown of thorns bushes
          (the plant's soft petals hiding
          its brutal spikes)
hold the cracks
in the terra-cotta tiles together.

And seated
on the edge of a fountain, small and lonely,
is Liora.

She's never looked less
like one of Yemaya's children.
The maid of spring and summer
is gone; this new girl
is a gust of February wind, sharp and white.
Her voice
sits in her throat, waiting to be used
for the Prince's pleasure
to bring another iris or monarch butterfly to life.

Liora whips around and her dress flickers—
a sparkler about to ignite.
*Who's there?* she asks,
all barbs, no softness.

I go first, Ariel held in front of me,
the promise of music
an offering and a shield.

*It's us, Liora.*
*Andres and Renee.*
*We've come to bring you*
*home.*

Liora turns from us,
a waning moon of a girl.
*I told you before—*
*I don't want to go!*
*This is my home!*
*I belong here.*

*You don't,* says Renee.
*I wish*
no one *belonged to this place, to their own regrets.*
*But you especially don't.*
*You're not* dead, *Liora.*

*I am!* Liora insists.

I never thought I'd see Renee beg anyone
for *anything.*
Even when she makes her requests
to the sea and storm gods, Yemaya and Oya,
I imagine she does it upright.
But she drops to her knees beside Liora,
a girl before an altar, an icon,
a star worth worshipping.
*Liora, I don't know*
*what happened to you in Miami.*

*I don't know*
*why you were out so late,*
*why you didn't see the car coming,*
*why you don't want to remember*
*Andres and me.*
*But if you stay here, this City*
*will drain your light.*
*Even if you won't come back for us,*
*come back for Saturday mornings, iced coffee,*
*pirouettes, sunlight streaming*
*through your bedroom window,*
*butterfly migrations.*
*Please, Liora.*
*Remember.*

With a creaking motion
suited for this land of rusted dreams,
Renee lifts her camera
toward our girlfriend.

*No!*
But Liora's protest
comes too late.
The camera's eye blinks
and the first photo (of many) appears.

> We can wipe our minds clean . . .
> but we can't scrub our experiences
> out of our souls.

# CHAPTER
## FORTY-TWO

**Animated by Liora's memories,**
the pictures
twist themselves into new shapes.
Few are beautiful; fewer are what I expect.

Here is the glare of a ballet teacher
as Liora falters on her toes,
the Cyclops eye of a bathroom scale
watching
as she shoves two fingers down her throat.
       (The goal is to be gossamer,
       to float
       instead of touching the sand.)
Here are Mrs. Rose's lectures striking Liora
like stones
at the dining room table, in the car,
at every opportunity she has.

*(Don't you want to have*
*a bright future?*
*Don't you want to have*
*what I wasn't able to?*
*Keep your grades up; be better*
*than the best, be better*
*than I was.*
*I'm giving you everything*
*I never had.*
*So*
*be*
*grateful!)*

But the memories
Liora looks away from entirely
are her last ones on earth.

**That night**

     (*this* night,

     because time is a broken watch in the underworld,

     forever two minutes to midnight),

Mrs. Rose stood over Liora, a bouquet of photographs
captured in her fists.

The pictures are my happiest moments
colliding
with Liora's worst.
They are the photos Renee took of our triad
at Vizcaya.

I recognize them all—
the tilt of a smile here,
a kiss placed on pink lips there.

(They never should have been weapons;
they're too gentle for that.)

*These pictures explain*
*the B+ in Algebra last semester,*
*all those days you spent at the beach*
*instead of the dance studio!* Mrs. Rose hollered.
*You don't have time*
*to be playing around*
*with some Latin hotshot, some goth girl!*
*You don't have time*
*to be warming their beds!*
*I expected better from you,*
*Liora Rose!*

Despair eroded Liora, shrinking her
till she was less than a City phantom.
*Mom, please!* Liora struggled to say.
*It's not like that.*
*I love them!*

Mrs. Rose threw the photos
at Liora's bare feet.
*You're sixteen!*

*You don't know what love is.*
*And it's not fooling around with two people*
*at the same time*
*because you can't make a choice!*
*End this, Liora!*
*Or I'll make you.*

My girlfriend's toes curled into the floor,
taking fifth position
on instinct.
Tears scalding in her eyes, she leaped
over the photos and past Mrs. Rose.

The night beckoned to her, promising
an escape.
Not even her mother's cries
could catch her
as she sprinted
through the open door, the garden

                       and onto

           the street.

I told Renee,
*Miami drivers are reckless.*
I told Renee,
*They think*
*they can outrace anything.*

I was right.
They tried to outrace a girl made of light.
And neither of them
won.

**Pain is every note in the body played at once;**
it overwhelms the senses.
And when the car struck Liora,
she felt *everything*.

Not even the Prince's kiss
could take that away.

# CHAPTER
## FORTY-THREE

**Deep in the underworld,**
Liora lets her dress slip from one shoulder,
a snake shedding old skin.
What's beneath it?
Ribs that stick out like spears,
a roadway of suffering,
the path of needles and pins
        (through the lost woods)
Renee warned me about.

What's the geography of sadness?
This moment,
stretched to the soul's breaking point.

Liora's truth spills free, a current
that can't be trapped anymore.
*I'm not all light*, she whispers.
*I'm not just the dawn.*

*I'm what comes before and after too.*
*But I wanted to be*
*perfect, luminous—*
*for you two, for my mother,*
*on the stage and at home.*
*But here in the City,*
*I don't need to be perfect.*


Liora grips Renee's hands so tightly
she steals the color from them.
*I remember everything now . . .*
*but I*

　　　　*don't*

　　　　　　*want to.*
*Please, Renee. Please, Andres.*
*Accept the Prince's kiss.*
*Your yesterdays would span minutes;*
*your tomorrows would be just hours.*
*You'd have no past to hurt you,*
*no future to worry about.*
*We could all finally be happy*
*in the present*
*because the present is the only thing*
*we'll ever have.*


I touch my finger to my lips.
The future is troubling; the past is an ache.
It's the present
I've always found the most joy in.
Could the Prince's kiss
grant me that?

But when I tried to discard my history,
its long shadows
tracked me down.

(Every drop of water
has to return to its source somehow.)

**I stand beside the mermaid girls,**
hoping to be a shelter
            (not a storm)
even as my shadows seem to growl,
*Give in*
*to the Prince and what he promises,*
*to the hopelessness*
*of the past and the future.*

But Ariel
            (my better half)
declares,
*What's the truest test of love?*
*Being able to hold on.*
*Being able to face someone else's pain*
*and not look away.*

I position my guitar
on my knees.
            (If I'm to worship anything, let it
            be love.)
Ignoring the bite of my black stars,
I play for Liora and Renee:

*I see your joy;*
*I see your despair.*
*I accept both, and I want to grow*
*with you*
*to new heights,*
*add new steps to our ballet,*
*new notes to our songs*
*in the book of me and you and you.*
*I want us to share*
*orange trees and slow, gentle mornings.*
*I want*
*the two of you*
*exactly as you are.*

**Liora crushes her fists to her tearstained eyes.**
*You won't want me*
*if I'm not perfect, if I'm weak,*
*if I don't keep smiling.*

*We will,* Renee promises.
She taps
two fingers against the spiderweb of scars
marking her left wrist.
*We all should wear our imperfections*
*more openly,*
*stop trying to shove them grave deep*
*in our bellies.*
She swings to me,
as much a dancer as Liora.

*We met a boy*
*named Virgil, named* Vasyl,
*who didn't hide his pain.*
*Some people recoiled from that.*
*But the ones who didn't*
*were the ones who* understood *him.*
*Or at least the ones*
*who wanted to try.*

Renee and I
lift Liora off the fountain's rim;
we lift our voices too.
*Ground Control*
*to Major Tom.*

Slowly, Liora takes a fallen photograph
off the ground.
I don't see which memory it is;
I don't need to.

What I need is Liora's answer . . .
and it comes
as her fingers catalogue my shadows, Renee's scars,
all of who and what we are.

*There must be a way out of here,* Liora says,
*for all three of us.*

# CHAPTER
## FORTY-FOUR

**No love song should be interrupted,**
but the Prince in the dark
has no respect for romance—
doomed, destined, or otherwise.
His applause is earsplitting, mocking;
it stamps out our melody midchorus.

I whip around and see him
leaning against the doorframe, a mockery of Virgil,
barring our road home.

The Prince's grin,
            (more smirk than smile)
could cut through barbed wire.
*No one's ever broken the spell*
*my kiss casts before*, he says.

*I almost have to admire*
*what you've done.*
*But it changes nothing.*
*Liora promised to stay here*
*in exchange for my kiss.*

Renee steps forward to meet the Prince
and all his lies.

      (And maybe,

        all his truths too.)

*Who* are *you?*

The Prince laughs.
*Oh, you know me.*
*And very well*
*at that.*
*Here—*
*let me show you.*

Before I can cry out
for him to stop, the Prince reaches up
and peels away
his hood.

And my own face

      stares

           back

              at me.

The Prince in the dark
the cancer in *me*,
the rot in every rose I've ever held,
is the boy
I would have stayed
if I'd kept trying to beat down the world
that almost ground me to dust.

I let go of my anger; I let go of *him*.
Yet here he is,
          alive,
               in the land
                    of the dead.

**Renee's fists curl like ropes of kudzu**
around Liora's.
*Andres. . . . What is this?*
*Why does* he
*look like* you?

The Prince doesn't let me answer
for myself.
        (Princes never do.)
*Because we used to be one*, he drawls.
*One boy, one voice, one life.*
*Until Andres left me*
*here to* rot.

*But it didn't take long for me*
*to understand*
*it was better to be the prince of Hell*
*than a servant in Heaven.*
           *(If you could call*
           *the world above* that.)

*This isn't Hell*, I snarl back.

The Prince slithers up to me, and I tense,
my hands at the ready.
If I can resurrect my old war songs,
can I cut down my own anger
molded into a boy, without being consumed
by it again?
Can I somehow beat the Prince
without *becoming* him?

*Heaven, Hell, Purgatory—*
*whatever you want to call this City,*
*it's still my kingdom*, the Prince says.
*The dead worship me,*
*because* before me,
*the River Lethe had all but dried up.*
*But I still had mouthfuls of our river*
*inside me—*
*the Tietê River that tried to drown us*
*when we threw ourselves into it,*
*looking for an escape.*
*And what better escape is there*
*than forgetting everything?*

The tragedy?
He's right.

**The Prince twines a lock of Liora's hair**
around his finger,
an unwilling wedding band.
*Go home,*
*light bringers*, he tells me and Renee.
*You can't take anything belonging to me*
*out of my kingdom.*

I strike his hand away
before Liora can.
*Liora isn't a possession!* I shout.
*You can't own another person!*

The Prince's cackle could shake the soul
to its roots.
*Nobody belongs solely to themself.*
*Everybody owes a debt to someone else:*
*a mother for birth, a father for half our genes,*
*a lover for a kiss, an enemy for a scar.*
*The world is transactional*
*by nature.*
*Why do we pretend*
*it's anything but?*

*That's such a sad way*
*of looking at the world*, Liora murmurs.

The Prince's smile slashes upward.
*Spoken like someone who's never been used*
*and thrown away.*

Renee is steady as the rain
outside the downside mansion
as she says:
*I have.*
*But in the abyss, I learned what you didn't:*
*being discarded by someone*
*said more about who they were*
*than it did about my worth.*

The Prince shrugs her insight aside
as he moves across the courtyard on his toes
like a child.
Underneath the spite and conjured glamor,
that's all he is—
a little boy, bleeding and dragging
everyone else with him
as he falls.

# CHAPTER
## FORTY-FIVE

**The Prince thrusts his arm deep**
into the crown of thorns bush
Liora's songs grew.
The sharpness of it suits him
more than the tender brush of its red petals.

The crown of thorns
shifts into a declaration of violence: a sword
hungry for blood.
Mind over matter, right?
And it's so damn easy to become a blade
in this place.

The Prince jabs his newly forged weapon
at me.
*I'll make you a deal, Andres—*
*since you like deals so much.*

*The price of Liora's freedom is winning*
*a fight*
*against me.*

My answer is automatic.
*No!*
*I won't fight you; I won't fight myself.*
*That isn't me anymore!*

*Coward!* spits the Prince.
*If you won't fight,*
*then Liora must stay with me.*
*She can't go back*
*on her word.*
*Words are all we have*
*here in the City; they're binding.*

Liora's head lolls forward.
*He's right—I made a promise.*
*And I can't let anyone get hurt*
*because of me again.*
Strands of golden hair
rustle against her cheeks, half muffling a cry.
        (Mermaids are like boys;
        they pretend to have no tears.)
Liora takes first position, second, third,
preparing herself to go
to the Prince.

I can't let her song
end here.
I pick up Ariel, my weapon of choice . . .
but will she be enough?

*If I win*, I say to the Prince,
*all three of us get to go home.*

The Prince traces a finger down his blade.
Its thorns don't dare prick his skin;
they must fear retaliation.
*I accept.*

*No.* Liora chokes—
on the Prince's kiss and the river
he holds inside him.

Renee follows, saying,
*Andres, wait—*

But the Prince *doesn't* wait
for her to finish.
He launches himself
                    at
                              me,
a splinter seeking soft skin.

I hold out my guitar, and my shadow's sword
CRASHES
onto the strings.

(To Ariel's credit, she stays

intact.)

*Ground Control*

*to Major Tom*, she calls to the Prince.


He doesn't listen.

He never does.


**We, shadow and caster, are both jaguars now,**

our claws out, our teeth displayed.

We're the approach of evening,

crushing the remaining daylight from the sky.


The Prince is strong—he survived

the same death I did, after all.

But his strength

is far from precise.

He lashes out in a frenzy,

hair and spittle flying

as we perform our terrible dance.

*I don't need*

*your kind seas, your love, your music!* the Prince hisses.

*I have a princess, a tower,*

*a weapon of my own now!*

*I have all the pieces*

*I need to slay you and let legends*

*hatch from your bones!*


Ariel refuses to play battle hymns,

no matter how viciously the Prince strikes

her neck, body, fingerboard.

If he's delirium, she's restraint.
And I'm between the two, my black stars
burning to my core.

Every blow
the Prince delivers makes my hands
sing with pain—
and my heart sing with anger.

But it's not the Prince
stoking my fury.
It's the world and the grown-ups who shaped him
driving the flames in me
higher and higher.

Whenever I had to cobble together
excuses for Papi
or dry Mami's tears
as she told me I was no better than him,
I had every right to be furious
with them.

Like the Prince has every right to be furious
with *me*.

What wells in me past exhaustion:
pity
for the Prince, the boy I was, all the boys
like us.

Other people dance the tarantella to draw
the poison out;
the Prince fights
in the hope of doing the same.

**The Prince's blade brushes my cheek**
with the passion of a lover, but I
don't
        stab
                back.

I catch his wrist, the way Virgil caught mine
in the crumbling theater.
*I'm done fighting you,* I say.
*But I won't let you keep Liora either.*
*She's not a crown*
*for you to wear;*
*she's a person*
*with dreams of her own.*
*Let her go, and I'll stay*
                *beside*
                    *you.*
*Because you're just as much a part of me*
*as the music, aren't you?*
*You were my armor, my protection.*
*You were the only means I had to save*
*myself.*

The Prince
withdraws into the silhouettes he's cut from,
sword and all.

He's a war of clashing feelings—
confusion to rage, rage to loneliness.

*Please*, I beg.
*I was wrong to abandon you.*
*Just like you'd be wrong to bind someone here*
*when they want to leave.*

The Prince tucks his sneer away with care,
like the carnival mask
it is.

> (What's under fury?
> Distress, loneliness, a union
> of the two.)

With aching slowness, he extends his hand
to me,
the skin of his palms
unmarked by months spent kindling music
on Ariel's strings.

> (I forget he's younger than I am,
> a lost boy in every sense).

*Promise then*, says my shadow, trembling.
*Promise me*
*you won't leave me alone*
*ever again.*

# CHAPTER
## FORTY-SIX

**I go to accept his hand—**
and Renee and Liora grab mine,
birds of paradise trying to contain a raven.

*No!* Liora cries.
*This is all my fault!*
*The two of you wouldn't be down here*
*if it weren't for me.*
*Please, leave me to the Prince*
*and this City.*

Neither *of you should be here!* Renee argues.
*We'll all find a way to end*
*these shadows together.*
*We'll find another road*
*out of the City, through Death's country,*
*hand in hand.*

*If there were another way*, I murmur,
*the City wouldn't exist.*
*It's the kingdom of regrets, remember?*
*But I'll regret so much more*
*if I let my shadow, my dark woods*
*swallow anyone else.*

My final love song
isn't one I can play on seven notes or six chords.
My last love song is an act,
as love should always be.
I kiss my girlfriends . . .
and pull my shadow into an embrace.

The Prince and I are two asteroids
meeting in the same stretch of sky.
My shadow and his river
thread through my ribs, my veins, the fractals of my spirit.
He's a weight
in the pit of my stomach,
a hawk's warning call in my mouth.

But he's not
        all
             I
                  am.

This knowledge expands in me,
a soap bubble, a web of colors.
It makes my feet rise off the tiles, Neverland bound.

I will never be left alone
with only the wounded places in myself
for company again.

And as they
      watch
      me
      soar,
Renee and Liora do the same.

              We are all free.

              (But even unbound and floating,
              Death still has dominion
              over this place . . .
              and me.
              Her whispers fill
        the halls of my mind, the depths of my shadow.

              *Come and find me*, Death says.
              *Come and pay me*
              *what you owe.*

# CHAPTER
## FORTY-SEVEN

**All souls are butterflies; ours are no different.**
With no remorse to weigh us down,
the three of us flutter
past the City's ashen souls,
its rain-doused rooftops,
the creature whose lonely bones
built its gates.

I thought we were a single ode
to a shared future.
But as we rise, Liora's soul drifts
farther from ours.
I strain
my darkness and my light
as far as either will extend, trying
to catch her.

It's Renee's voice that stills both.
*Liora has to find her body*
*in the hospital;*
*she has to settle into her skin again.*

*And what if Mrs. Rose is there*
*when she wakes up?*
*What if she tries to talk Liora*
*out of love again?* I counter.
*Out of being* herself?

*Then we have to trust*
*Liora will talk her way*
*back into it*, says Renee.
*We have to trust*
*she won't walk away*
*from us, from everything she is.*
*We have to trust* her.

# CHAPTER
## FORTY-EIGHT

I
        slam
               back
                        into
**my own body.**
        (Shadow and all.)
The water that greets me
washes away
the petrichor perfume of the underworld.

This time,
there are no paramedics, doctors, parents
begging me to stay tucked in my bones.
There's only Renee,
her sopping hair undone
on her shoulders,
and the sunlight conquering my vision.

It transforms the upside of Vizcaya
        (no spirits to be seen
        in the fortress of banyan trees)
to molten gold.

I wipe
beads of water from my cheeks.
They're not tears . . . but they could be.
*Did we do it?* I ask.
*Is Liora awake?*

Renee plucks me from the fountain.
*Let's go and find out.*

**This time, we don't need Ariel's magic to help us**
navigate the hospital's winding halls.
We already know the seven floors
we have to cross,
just like seven turns
we made in Vasyl-Virgil's home.

We shove past
doctors, nurses, the occasional police officer,
twin smiles riding out mouths.
If the underworld couldn't stop us,
it's laughable
any adult would even try.

But it's an adult we have to confront
when we reach Liora's room.

**Liora is a flower battered by the winter,**
Eurydice who has taken her first stumbling steps
out of the underworld.
She's still as translucent as a ghost;
the bandages and the cast
keeping her left arm in place
are still too close to shrouds for comfort.

But her eyes are open,
and they're not the color of rain
or buildings razed by ancient wars.
Liora
                is
                            *alive*
and here with us.
*Renee*, she whispers.
*Andres.*

Mrs. Rose's anger makes her swift.
She springs from her daughter's bedside, snarling,
*What did I tell you two*
*about coming here?*
*You aren't welcome*
*near Liora!*

The Prince starts to bear his own teeth—
and mine respond in kind.

> (*She can't talk to us like that!* he hollers.
> *We're only here*
> *because we love her daughter!*
> *How*
>
> > *dare*
> >
> > > *she!*)

But I don't need to soothe my shadow.
It's Liora
who propels him back.
*They* are *welcome*, she tells Mrs. Rose.
*I want them*
*here with me, Mom.*

Mrs. Rose speeds on,
as if her daughter hadn't spoken.
(The opinions of grown-ups
hold more weight
than any stretch of sea.)
*I know what the two of you*
*have been doing with my daughter!*
*Tricking her into thinking you love her*
*when it's obvious*
*you want one thing*
*and one thing only*
*from her!*

If it weren't for the parade of doctors
passing the room in a white stream,
I believe Mrs. Rose would unleash
the insults
poised on the tip of her tongue:
*Playboy* and *slut*, *predator* and *witch*.

Liora sits up
a little straighter, transforming herself
into a tower of a girl.
*Renee and Andres aren't monsters;*
*they aren't manipulating me.*
*They* love *me.*
*And they don't expect me to be perfect.*
She heaves out a breath, heavy with the life
she's fought to return to.
*I'm not perfect, Mom.*
*Maybe I can't be the daughter*
*you want me to be.*
*Maybe I can't look a certain way,*
*or do all the things* you *wanted to do*
*when you were my age.*
*I can just be myself: perfectly* imperfect.
*And whether you accept me*
*won't change*
*who I am.*
Liora looks to Renee and me, smiling.
*It won't change*
*who I love either.*

There's a softness in Renee's answering grin
as she tugs her camera off and sets it
on Liora's bedside.
She's come without her armor—
and she wants us all to know it.

Renee tells Mrs. Rose,
*You should be proud*
*you raised someone*
*who has so much room inside her*
*for other people and their dreams.*

*But we all need to make space*
*for Liora's dreams too,* I say.
*For all of her.*
*Even the parts*
*we might sometimes disagree with.*
*Even the parts that hurt us to look at*
*because we know*
*they're hurting* her.
*That's what loving someone* means.

Shame blooms
in Mrs. Rose's cheeks and she falls
silent.

Exposing your soul
is never easy.
But I'm glad Liora's done it.

I'm glad *we've* done it.
And I'm glad her mother
knows her truth.

**Does Mrs. Rose embrace us, after?**
Does she declare
Renee her second daughter, me her new son?

No.
But she doesn't drive us out either.
She sits with what Liora told her,
letting it shrink her anger
to a dying ember.
She sits with us too.

        (Acceptance comes
        in small steps.)

Our triad doesn't mention
the Prince, the City, the souls there;
no earthly words can describe them.
Instead, we soak in life, one another's company,
comfortable silence.

And at the end of visiting hour,
Renee and I kiss Liora,
mindful of the cuts on her mouth,
the bruise on her cheek.
She's not bleeding light anymore.

But we know it's inside her,
waiting for the chance to shine.
*We'll come back tomorrow*, we promise.
*And the next day, and the day after.*

*Andres wants to paint you rainbows*, Renee adds.
*He wants to give you all the colors*
*you were missing.*
*And I'm going to hold him*
*to that.*

**With the sun moving steadily higher**
in the mid-morning sky,
I know I'll have to make my way
home soon.
I'll have to face what's waiting there
for me and my shadow—
whether that's Mami's sobs or Papi's (false) bravado.
We'll have to learn
how to be *whole*.

But first, I have a debt to pay.
Whatever shape that payment
may take.

# CHAPTER
# FORTY-NINE

**No one has removed**
the seven cigarettes, the seven squares of chocolate,
the scattering of flower petals
from the rim of the fountain at Vizcaya,
where Renee laid them
so long ago.

        (And only last night.)


The security guards must have known offerings
when they saw them.
And who would be foolish enough to rob
eternity itself?


As I kneel before the ofrendas,
Death's voice and the scent of her roses
replace the rain still thundering
somewhere
in the far reaches of my mind.

*Tell me, little prince, little musician . . .*
*what is it*
*you love?* Death asks.

Ariel and I don't give her a lament.
We give her a story.
*I love the sound of the sea;*
*I love sunsets and my new city*, I sing.
*I love Liora; I love Renee.*
*I love that the future*
*will be different from the past.*
*And I love . . .*

Here, I falter.
But Ariel coaxes out my next refrain,
like she's known all along
what we came here to do.

*Say goodbye*, she whispers,
*so you can say hello*
*to the world again.*
*Who is Orpheus without his lyre?*
*Still a musician; still himself.*

I swallow the stone
that's rolled into my throat
and place my guitar
            (my payment, my sacrifice)
at the base of the fountain.

*I love Ariel*, I tell Death.
*Because she brought me*
*those other moments,*
*allowed me to connect with my girlfriends,*
*and find the means to reforge*
*the feelings that gnawed at me*
*day in and day out.*
*So Ariel*
*is what I give you now.*

Death's smile and her scythe are one,
just . . . and merciful.
*I accept your payment*, she says.
*The night is over, little prince, little musician.*
*Your new day awaits.*

**I leave Vizcaya empty-handed.**
But the once-empty places in *me*
are full of dawn fire, frustration, devotion,
*hope*.

There are many ways to be
a boy, a man, *myself*.
I'll be fierce when it's necessary;
there are times when my anger
(at my parents, at the injustices of the world)
will be warranted.
I'll be gentle as often as I can;
there are times when a song
will be the best defense I have.

My shadow and I
stand in our new truths—
imperfect, perfectly us.

My name is Andres Santos,
and I believe
I have more love
than darkness
to give.

**THE END**

# ACKNOWLEDGMENTS

Thank you to my editor, Ashley Hearn, for your endless enthusiasm and for always bringing out the best in my characters and prose.

Thank you to the publicity and design team at Peachtree and Holiday House, for their tireless efforts to make this book as beautiful and accessible to readers as possible.

Thank you to Rena Rossner, my fellow Miamian, for loving this story and putting it in the best hands.

Thank you to Jacob, the Eurydice to my Orpheus (or is it reversed?), for never letting me brave the underworld alone. And thank you to Peter for being there for us both.

Thank you to Celeste Gleason, who knows what it's like to venture into the dark.

Thank you to River and Etienne, who listened to the story of my descent without flinching.

Thank you to the real Virgil, for never taking my nonsense.

Thank you to my family, for ending my reign as the Typo Queen and sending me cat memes when I needed them.

Thank you to Kip, Alex, Roselle, Celyta, Li, Steven, Andrzej, and Bridget for their friendship, and to all the readers and book bloggers who have supported my work over the years.

Thank you to Henry VIII, the best cat. You have the brain cell more often than the other oranges. (But don't tell them I said that.)

And finally, thank you to David Bowie, the alien unseelie prince. This world misses you, but I hope you're enjoying your time as ruler of the Goblin Kingdom.

# ABOUT THE AUTHOR

**R. M. ROMERO** is a Jewish Latina and author of fairy tales for children and adults. She lives in Miami Beach with her cat, Robin Goodfellow, and spends her summers helping to maintain Jewish cemeteries in Poland. You can visit her online at *RMRomero.com.*